MIKE TYSON SLEPT HERE ——————————+

MIKE TYSON SLEPT HERE

Chris Huntington

Boaz Publishing Company

To Shasta, a good thing who has stayed that way,
and Dagim, the best thing of all

Address all inquiries to:
Boaz Publishing Company
968 Ordway Street
Albany, CA 94706
www.boazpublishing.com
info@boazpublishing.com
(510) 220 6336

Cover design by Elizabeth Vahlsing
Book Design by BookMatters

Manufactured in the United States of America

Library of Congress Cataloging-in-Publication Data
Huntington, Chris, 1967–
   Mike Tyson slept here / Chris Huntington.
      p.   cm.
   ISBN 978-1-893448-10-0
   I. Title.
PS3608.U59498M55   2011
813'.6—dc22   2011009381

CONTENTS

BRANT GILMOUR:
What I Learned in Prison

I WAS TWENTY-TWO, teaching GED classes at the prison Mike Tyson made famous. My best friend on the job was a guy named Englehart, who outweighed me by about sixty pounds and wore the stretched, deep-pocketed uniform of a "corrections officer." He wasn't the first officer to tell me he wasn't a guard. "What am I guarding?" he asked. "Look around! This ain't exactly the fucking White House."

Unlike a lot of officers, Englehart had a college degree, but he wasn't vain about it. According to Englehart, Indiana State was where Larry Bird had gone to school after losing his job as a garbage man. Englehart considered going to school in Terre Haute as "college for people too stupid to pass their SATs, but too fat to join the army."

Like a lot of rude people, Englehart said he was just being honest.

One morning, I heard Englehart say to an inmate: "I'm sure being locked up here is a bad way to spend your birthday, I'm sure it is. But there's a reason you're in the universe's digestive tract."

"What's that?"

Englehart paused. "You're shit."

One time I asked Englehart what he'd studied at Indiana State. "Criminal justice," he said. "Isn't that an oxymoron?"

"No. Well, I call it a contradiction."

He nodded. "You were an English major, weren't you, Gilmour?"

"Yeah."

"I knew it."

"Look," I said. "Why do you always play the redneck? We both know you've been to school."

"Sure, I been to school. But the question ain't why I act like I do. The question is: why do you act the way you do? Why do you try and talk like NP-fucking-R? You think you're something special?"

"Yeah. Here's how special I am. Pull my finger."

Englehart laughed. "Fuck you," he said. But he meant that in the best way, which was that he wanted to be friends.

"Why don't you teach in a real school?" Englehart asked me. "Why you want to work here?"

I looked at him. "Why do you want to work here?"

"Man, I don't. I sure as hell don't. I just need the experience. Then I'm going IPD. Be an officer. You ever see *COPS*? That's what I want to do. Drive around and shine the light on people in the middle of the night. If I have to, I'll go county and be a sheriff's deputy. I don't care. But

I'm getting out of here. That's my plan. You? What about you?"

"I like to feel needed," I said.

"Needed? These guys don't need you. They're using you. You think people sell crystal meth because they don't know how to do fractions? How is a GED gonna stop one of these guys from touching little kids? Needed? Shit. These guys need a kick in the ass. All you're doing, you're making drug dealers who can spell."

I smiled. "Well, in that case, I'm doing it for the experience."

But that night Englehart came by my room when I was locking my file cabinets and getting ready to go home.

"Hey," he said from the doorway. "You know what I said before? About making a difference? You just keep at it, man. Yeah. Someone's got to."

Englehart got fired for trafficking five months later. He was bringing tobacco into the facility. He'd pack a ziplock bag of it at the bottom of his McDonald's cup, then pour ice and Diet Coke on top. Make a quick fifty bucks.

One time in the parking lot, Englehart had asked me what the difference was between a corrections officer and an inmate, since both spent all day looking at the same fence. "The tattoos?" I said. "Teeth?"

"No," he said. "We just do our sentences eight hours at a time."

After he got fired, I called him at home. We talked for about ten minutes before awkwardly hanging up.

"You know," he said, "when I started working there, I never thought I'd get mixed up in shit, you know? Never. I was going to make a difference. Like you. You ought to quit. Seriously. If you stick around there, you won't be a nice guy anymore—you know that, Gilmour? You know what I learned in prison, man?"

"What?"

"You're in the barber shop long enough, sooner or later you're going to get a haircut." He paused a moment. "Wait and see."

BRANT GILMOUR AND ISA BOONE
Part 1

When I first got to the prison, I was nervous as a newlywed. Isa Boone made me feel at home by making fun of my pants.

"Dockers. Nice," she said. "Your mom buy those for you?" She pointed me toward a plastic dish for my wallet and car keys. I arranged the tub like it was a little boat on a conveyor belt river and watched it go through the X-ray machine. An officer patted me down efficiently, finding a pack of gum. I was embarrassed, but he handed it back to me.

Isa pulled her bookbag on wheels. It was like we were going to catch a plane together, but of course we were simply heading deeper into the prison where I would teach GED classes. Isa was thirty-two, but she had a smile half her age: full of unwise mischief. She wasn't bad looking, but she wasn't really good looking either. She had bony shoulders, a flat chest, and a big ass. To be brutally honest, she had a magical face, but her ass was unusually large, like the asses of two people, really. Still, it was my first day in the prison and I hadn't expected to fall in love.

"Brant Gilmour," I said, holding out my hand. Isa pumped it quickly, a boylike, embarrassed handshake.

"Heard you were starting. Your first job?"

"I student-taught at Bloomington South. Should I be worried?"

"Only that you'll work here twenty years. Have you met Carlson yet? He's worked here thirty-four years. Teaching got him a deferment from going to Vietnam. He's never worked anywhere else. Couldn't, really. He couldn't work with kids now if you gave him a job handing out Hershey bars. He can't relate to normal people."

"Really?"

"He's institutionalized. It can happen to anyone."

The rollers on Isa's bookbag suitcase made a droning, brainless sound on the tile floor. We were at the sally port before I realized it was my turn to speak.

"Relax." Isa shook my arm. "I was kidding."

It was my first job out of college and I wanted to do it well. But I was also scared—of all the people around me, of all the khaki uniforms standing in crooked lines on the sidewalks, the men with wrinkled faces staring at the parking lot and the state highway in the distance. It was strange to see a chain-link fence ten feet inside another chain-link fence. Isa ignored it all. She wore makeup and was lightly fragrant. I was glad she was a woman. It made me feel I was still in college, not in a prison. And because she walked with me, I felt as though she liked me, which was not a feeling I had as I looked away from the bad haircuts and the silent men standing outside the mail room. And these were just the guards.

I didn't do anything particularly complicated with my students that first day. I just introduced myself and passed out books, which they had to sign for. I had an old desk with an ancient computer and a dot matrix printer. A chalkboard. No chalk, but the secretary told me this was on order. I decided I could stop later and spend a dollar fifty of my own; that didn't seem like too much to pay to be a good teacher. After class I walked around the room and imagined myself in it for the next few years. Then I realized that someone had stolen all the unlined paper out of my printer. The students had legal tablets, but I'd been warned they liked blank paper for drawing.

I waved good-bye to Isa across the parking lot as we left that afternoon. She was talking on her cell phone. I sat in my car and reached into my coat pocket for my chewing gum. It was gone. My coat had been on the chair behind my desk all day. I'd been told in training that I had to be careful because inmates rarely made their play as soon as they met you.

"They've got time," my trainer had said. "They'll size you up for a few weeks. Maybe months. Then they'll spin you."

But with me, I guessed, they'd realized they had no need to wait. I was too young. Too stupid. Maybe they figured I wouldn't last a month. Someone punked me the first few hours, walked right past me with an inch of typing paper underneath his T-shirt. And someone else had stolen my gum from my coat pocket.

And that bothered me so much I felt sick to my stomach. It bothered me. Not for the few pennies it would take to replace the paper. Not for the Denta-Ice gum I'd lost. But because the inmates had so little respect for me. I'd entered a world of men, and they took me for a boy.

When I'd told my father I was going to teach in a prison instead of a pubic school, he said, "Brant, I know you think you're going to save the world, but let me ask you this: what are you going to do if you don't save the world? If, at the end of the day, the earth is still screwed up? What if, after you've spent your adult life locked up among rapists and drug dealers, you realize that this is your life? With them? It's a bottom feeder job; you don't trade up from this kind of thing. You don't make good contacts working in a prison. And you won't see results. Join the Peace Corps like you wanted to before. See the world! Work with kids! That's where the hope is. Don't do this, son! Because there's a very good chance you'll fail, Brant. Some people are just bad and you can't do anything about it. And I know you: when you fail, you'll feel like a failure in every atom of your body. I'm telling you this for your own good, Brant. I know you, god-damn it."

My father is not a very inspirational speaker, in my opinion. But maybe he's different at work. He sells cars.

Plainfield Correctional Facility was a medium-security prison outside of Indianapolis, and it housed "non-violent" offenders, including drug dealers, housebreakers, and sex offenders. All these crimes seemed steeped in violence to me, but there was no one to argue the point with. My job was to help inmates interested in earning their GEDs. During my first week, one of my students came to class with an eye that had gone bloodshot overnight. I don't mean a little pink. I mean it looked like a peeled tomato. He tried to hide it by tilting his head for most of the morning, and when I saw it he said he'd fallen in the shower. I sent him to the HCU (health care unit), and he wasn't very happy about it. He was mad.

"That makes no sense," I said to him. "Why the hell wouldn't you want to see a nurse? Your eye is bleeding inside."

"You wouldn't understand," he said.

At lunchtime I found Isa and another co-worker, Liz Cady, and told them the story. "I wouldn't understand?" I said. "Understand what? Explain it to me, please. Why not go to the doctor?"

"You ought to explain it to me," Isa said.

"Why?"

"It's so obviously a guy thing."

Liz Cady leaned back on the cinderblock wall, nudged Isa. "Not really. You know how you get."

"It's not a guy thing. It's a stubborn thing," I said.

"That's right." Liz Cady nodded, poked Isa again. "Isa, it's a stubborn thing."

"An ignorant thing." Isa snorted. "A guy thing. God, can we talk about something else? I spend fifty-five minutes an hour talking about guy things with guys."

"Come on now," I said. "Talking about people you don't like can be so much fun . . ."

Isa laughed. "Oh, you're going to fit right in here, all right. I can see that now."

Friday morning Isa asked me if I wanted to go out for a beer after work: "Your first Friday! You can tell me how much you hate it here."

"But I don't hate it. I like it here."

"In that case, you can listen to me." Then Isa described a place called Heavy's Parlor on Highway 40. People from work went there sometimes, Isa said, or rather, they used to, "before they all got middle aged."

"All right," I said. "Will you buy me a beer?"

"You should buy me a beer. Pump me—" she paused, "—for information."

"I can do that."

"How about we meet there? Can you find it? Otherwise people might talk."

"What people?"

She blinked. "Well, I meant our co-workers," she said, "but I understand your confusion."

When I arrived at Heavy's Parlor, Isa was already sitting at the end of the bar beside the video poker game. I took the stool next to her. A middle-aged bartender had the buttons of his shirt pressed up against the wood as he served her a Bud Lite. The space behind the bar was a little tight for him. Isa was the only customer there, and she looked relieved when I came in. We sat there for three beers and the place started to fill with noise and Carhartt jackets. Isa was still the only woman there. Even though she claimed to be above gossip, she gave me the whole story on Liz Cady, our fifty-three-year-old co-worker who was sleeping with a married man. Liz was divorced and lived alone. The married man lived two counties away but they met secretly at conferences and he was somehow a regular fixture in her hot tub. They were both over 200 pounds. Isa described the situation as "repugnant on every level, really; I imagine them in her backyard with the hot tub boiling and a bunch of hungry cannibals in the bushes throwing bay leaves into the water."

"How do you know all this?" I asked.

"Liz tells everyone. You're just always in your classroom preparing things. You should quit preparing lessons."

"Then how would I teach? Without lessons?"

"Didn't you get John Martin John in class this week?"

"Yeah."

"So how're your plans working out?"

John Martin John was sixty years old and could only read about one hundred words, including *stop* and *railroad crossing*. "We've just started," I said.

"You taught him to read yet?"

"It's only been five days."

"I give it five weeks," Isa said. "Then you'll be in the hallway telling dirty jokes and pencil-poking like the rest of us."

"Goofing off, you mean?"

"Five weeks," she said, holding up her fingers.

Between classes the next week, Isa asked me why I wanted to teach in a prison instead of in a public school, and I said, "To make a difference. Does that sound stupid?"

"I don't know. A difference in what?"

"I think we need to help people once they've been locked up. You know. Not just warehouse them in a big concrete and metal cage."

"I see," Isa said. "You think the penal system is dysfunctional, and so you want to make things better by being part of it."

"Well, I want to make things better."

"I'm only asking because, on one hand, I agree with you a hundred percent. But how is putting in a new minute hand going to fix a stopped clock?"

I could see students coming up the hall. "Well, even a stopped clock is right twice a day. I want to be there when that happens."

Isa nodded and turned toward her own classroom. Then, over her shoulder, she called out, "Don't blink."

As a routine, I would come into the hallway just before classes arrived. As the students began to saunter down the hallway, Isa would sigh and turn back to her room. "Back to the coal mine," she'd say. She talked tough, but I'd also come into her classroom and found her helping a student write a birthday card. She joked her students out of their seats and up to the chalkboard, got them to cover the wall with math problems. "Here's my basic lesson plan," she said.

"First I make them learn the times tables. I don't let them off the hook. We build on that. Then I act like someone who's not irritated to see them. I figure if I can do that at least, then I'm helping these guys. Some of them will never get their GEDs, but at least they can feel like not everyone in the human race hates them."

"That's good."

"Yeah, well, some days, I deserve an Academy Award."

"Jesus, Isa. Why do you teach here, if you hate it so much?"

"I like to feel sexy."

I knew that men watched her in the prison—across the yard, down the hall. It was like an unsaid, magnetic thing: a woman under fifty, standing among incarcerated men. Isa joked about it, but in the same way a bald man jokes about haircuts. It was a little wishful. It made me sad, because even Englehart, an officer I liked, once said about Isa: "Great, isn't she? Shame about that ass." I pretended not to understand, so he added, "She's got the ass of a two-hundred-pound truck driver. Don't tell me you haven't noticed."

One day, a nurse crossing the yard drew two students to the window and, because they'd completely forgotten about us, Isa and I both heard one of them say, "Check out the titties on that little bitch; I'll bet her back kills her at night."

"She got to sleep on her side," another inmate said. "Got to. On account of she might suffocate if one of them fell on her face."

Isa rolled her eyes. We moved away from the wall.

"Nice, isn't it?" I said. "In the spring, when a young man's thoughts turn to love?"

Isa snorted. "If you've ever worked a public school, you should know that this is nothing compared to what junior high girls will say. No, I'm happy enough here. I'll never teach public school again."

I had what I felt was a breakthrough with John Martin John a few days later, and I found Isa in her classroom to tell her about it: "I said 'Mr. John, you just come to class every day, okay? We'll read one chapter a day out loud. We do this every day for two months. How can you not be a better reader at the end? It'd be impossible.' And he started smiling ear-to-ear. I think I'm the first teacher in his life who ever made him believe he can do something."

"Yes. That's nice."

"It's better than nice. It's why we teach, isn't it? What are you mad about?"

"Nothing."

"What?"

She mimicked me: "*How can you not be a better reader at the end?*' I just wish you wouldn't say stuff like that."

"Why not? It got him fired up."

"Look, you're not the first teacher around here to have John Martin John in class. And you are never going to last around here unless you get it into your head that it is never impossible for these guys to fuck up a good thing."

The next day I told Isa that what she'd said was still bothering me, but she interrupted me: "Look, maybe I was out of line. I just don't say stuff like you did anymore."

"Why?"

"You'll see," she said. "It's just too depressing when they fail."

Englehart didn't work the school building on a regular basis, but I saw him often. He developed a habit of stopping by my classroom and sniffing it, as though inmates were hiding there after hours. He saw me talking to Isa one time and stuck his head in. "What'd you teach them today, Professor?"

"Englehart," Isa said. "You're too late for today. He's already explained silent *e*. Maybe next time."

"Very funny."

We sat around on the tables for a few minutes, then Isa sauntered back to her own classroom. Englehart watched her go out the door, then shook his head and looked at me.

"What?"

"It's a shame."

"What?"

"What they say."

"About her ass? I don't even want to hear it, man. I don't."

Englehart looked at me in confusion. "No, guy. About her. What happened."

"What are you talking about?"

Englehart glanced at the door, then the ground, then at me.

"Tell me," I said. "You know I'll find out sooner or later. Around this place."

"Well, shit. It wasn't me who told you, okay?"

"Whatever you say."

"I just heard." He got up and shut the door to the hallway. "They say about four years ago she went down on some guy. An inmate. She was under investigation. But in the end she threatened a huge harassment charge and got the old director of education to back down. But they say. He was her classroom worker. Ask around about Raymond Avery."

Englehart opened the door. "Or don't ask," he said. "It's all the same to me."

The student we always joked about, John Martin John, was sixty years old and had somehow recently been sentenced to five years for animal cruelty, though what he'd done could have been described as an act of love. It involved a chicken and a Motel 6, which Liz Cady thought was just wonderfully sad. "He got it a hotel room," she said.

"Maybe he was living there," Isa said.

"No, he lives with his mother. He's always lived with her." Liz said. She had worked in the system for eight years and known John Martin John for six of them. His latest five-year bit was really just an "etc. etc." on a life filled with humiliations. He always reapplied to come to school, but he would probably never get his GED.

"I can't imagine the evidence table at his trial," Isa said. "That poor chicken."

"He should have eaten it," Liz said. "Then there wouldn't have been any evidence."

"You're not allowed to cook in a Motel 6," I said, which made the two women burst out laughing. The bell sounded and we separated in the hallway. "I'm not even sure how a man, could physically—you know—a chicken," I said to Isa. "John Martin John knows something I don't."

"Ah! The teacher so eager to learn from his students!" Isa said. "Just buy me a few drinks some time. Maybe I'll show you."

I turned to look at her, but she had stepped away, laughing, into her class.

I got to Heavy's Parlor first that Friday. I was halfway through a Bud Lite when Isa came through the door. "Sorry," she said. "I had to go by CVS."

"No problem." I noticed she had changed watches, of all things; she looked a little different from work. "You wearing makeup?"

"It's the weekend. I'm back to being me."

"All through the week people dress up for work. But on the weekend they dress how they see themselves. It's fun to see."

"And here you are, still in Dockers."

"You're harassing my pants again? Give me a break. I haven't been home yet."

"Buy me a beer."

I gestured to the bartender, who slouched off his stool

and pulled a bottle from the cooler without turning away from the opened sports pages on the bar.

Isa was ten years older than me, but when I asked her if she'd ever been married, she said, "Not even close."

"Why not?"

"Because I've got a big ass." Isa smiled at the mouth of her bottle. Her eyes caught mine. "Don't look, you bastard."

"Aw, you look all right," I said. "Shame about the mileage though. Thirty-two!"

"Yeah, right."

We had a beer apiece and decided to trade embarrassing stories. I told her a story about college—about streaking sorority houses and running into my sister, who was fifteen and attending science camp on campus that summer.

"Was that your most embarrassing moment or hers?"

"Both, probably." I took a drink. "You got one?"

Isa turned her watch around her wrist. "When I was ten years old, I didn't have many friends at school. I told these girls in my class that I was getting a Cabbage Patch Kid and they were all jealous. This was when the Cabbage Patch Kids were new. It was the first time anyone ever asked to come to my house. They all wanted to see my doll. And then days went by and I didn't get one. I begged my mother, but she said they were too expensive. The girls at school asked me to bring it to school, but I said my parents wouldn't let me. They all knew I was lying. Everyone knew."

When Isa glanced at her watch and said she had to get

moving, I reached out and touched her elbow. "Don't go. One more."

She smiled and seemed to think about it. "Friday night," she said. "A girl's not always free to drink for three, four hours straight after work. Maybe next time."

When she left the bar, we smiled good-bye to each other and I noticed again, the unfortunate way she was shaped. I also noticed the bartender looking up from his sports page, watching her, his lips moving thoughtfully. The door closed behind her and he went back to reading.

I went out with a girl I knew from I.U. that Saturday. Pearl had a museum-quality look because her parents had money, and she was blessed with great skin. She was down-to-earth, but it was obvious in talking to her that her father didn't sell cars for a living. She was volunteering at the Wheeler Mission. She drove the homeless van that collected the old, weak people who blew like yellow newspaper against fences in the wintertime. She took them to the shelter. She wanted to know all about prison life.

"Are you in danger?" she asked. We'd gone to a bar called the Old Point, where a sinister, tattooed bartender seemed to pour slowly at the mention of prison. He watched me a moment, then turned away in boredom.

"I'm not really in danger. My students could kill me, I guess. But why would they?"

"That's what I say." Pearl laughed. "To my parents. About the Mission visitors."

"Yeah."

Pearl put her chin on top of her hands. "But what you do is so—I don't know. I'm not going to say 'noble,' but it's really giving. More than just driving a car."

"Not really." I felt there was a chance that if I came up with a good enough story about prison, something sad and earned, it would have the strange effect of making Pearl sleep with me. The prospect was something I'd wanted the entire year and a half I'd known her, but now it seemed a bit sad and contradictory. I had an image of my hands clutching the small of her back and her mouth finally on top of mine, but a look of painful melancholy on both our faces. Something in me resisted. I told her about John Martin John, how we'd all had a good laugh in class when he was reading and kept saying "ON" when he came to the word "OFF."

"But Mr. John, how do you read the light switch?" I'd asked him.

I imitated his voice: "'ON is when it points up,' he said. 'Everybody knows that. And you been to college?'"

Pearl took a drink of beer. "I don't think it's very nice of you, laughing at that poor man's problem."

"Oh, come on. He was laughing, too."

"Imagine how he feels. He was probably just embarrassed."

"The guy fucked a chicken," I said. "Everybody knows it. I'm not saying we're all friends now, but he's not embarrassed about the little stuff like we're talking about."

"He what a chicken?"

"He didn't eat it. I'm sorry. Can we talk about something else?"

"Anything," Pearl said. "Please."

I asked Pearl to tell me an embarrassing story, and she demurred, saying, "You first." I told her my story about streaking on the I.U. campus, but all she said was, "You would not believe how many guys got drunk and ran across our lawn."

"You were a Tri-Delt, weren't you?" I said. "I forgot."

"I was."

"My sister just pledged," I said. "She's pretty proud of it."

"What is she?"

"Same as you. Delta Delta Delta."

"So she's my little sister."

"Hey, if my little sister is your little sister, that means you and I are—"

"That doesn't make us anything," Pearl said. She smiled.

Later Pearl and I walked up Mass Ave. to the tiny house she was renting. It was in streetlamp Lockerbie, the neighborhood where James Whitcomb Riley once lived and which was now brick sidewalks and ivy. The moon seemed caught in the tree branches as we bumped along beside each other, hands in our pockets, elbows touching.

At her doorstep I tried to kiss her, and she leaned her forehead into my mouth. "I'm sorry," she said, stepping away.

"I think you're nice, Brant. Really. You're a good person. I'm just not ready for anything right now."

"I'm not that nice," I said.

She smiled weakly. "You know, you asked me before about my most embarrassing moment?"

I nodded.

She smiled wide, then looked at her feet.

"Well." I smiled. "Imagine how I feel."

Liz Cady closed her desk drawer as I came into the room, but I could still smell chocolate. Liz and I were assigned to team-teach a class on being "long-distance dads" even though I didn't have kids of my own and Liz was obviously not a father. "Our qualifications?" I'd asked when we were given the class.

"We can read the syllabus." Liz held up a state document. "And we have some common sense."

As we waited for our students to arrive, I looked around the classroom. "Say, Liz, who was Raymond Avery?"

"Raymond Avery? I don't know. Why? Should I know him?"

"He used to work here? A clerk—tutor or something?"

"Oh—Avery! I didn't know his first name. Yeah, he used to be Isa's clerk or something. You heard about that?"

"I heard something."

"It's one of those things. You know. But I heard security found the two of them in a closet and she had dirt on the knees of her slacks. She said she'd been in there getting

Xerox paper and a stack fell on her. He supposedly rushed in to see if she was okay and the door shut."

"Really."

"Investigation cleared it. But Avery quit or got fired or something. Doesn't work here anymore. I think he might still be locked up somewhere."

"Do you believe that story?"

"Well, I've never been attacked by photocopy paper. And it's not like the wind slammed the door shut; we're in a brick building. But you never know . . . I like Isa. I just don't trust her."

One of the benefits about working in a prison is you can get free haircuts. I'd never worked up the nerve to get one because I was reasonably sure I would look like an inmate if I did. I'd started going to a stylist on 86th Street, the part of Indianapolis with a lot of Hummers and a Saks Fifth Avenue store. My stylist weighed maybe a hundred and thirty pounds and had blond highlights in his hair. Reed looked, to my eyes, cosmopolitan—whereas the prison barbers looked the other big-city word; they looked urban. The prison barbers were inmates with buzz cuts or fades that didn't always hide the tattoos on their skulls. They looked narrow-eyed and indifferent as you walked by the chair.

One day as I was passing the barber shop, a large, dark-skinned barber turned around so he was framed perfectly in the observation window. I saw the words "Avery, Raymond" on his ID.

I went in. "How about a haircut?" I said.

"Sure." The barber glanced from empty chair to empty chair. "I'm free."

He said the last without obvious inflection, though the irony was not lost on me. He took a position behind one chair and held up an apron. I sat, and he tucked the apron around my neck. "What'll it be?"

"Just a trim."

"Love a little trim," he said. "Don't you?"

Again, I could not tell by his expression just what he was saying. He watched me in the mirror as he un-drawered a comb and scissors. "How long have you been cutting hair?" I asked.

"Don't worry, sir. I know what I'm doing. I got my license a year ago. Mr. Scottie taught me. Over at the school."

"You were in the barbering program? I just started teaching there. The GED program."

He nodded.

"You get a GED there too?"

"No, sir."

Maybe if I hadn't hesitated, just a second, I could have simply asked him: did you ever work in the classrooms? But I didn't. I was watching his hands in the mirror. He held my hair delicately, but with a kind of authority. He didn't do the vaguely sculptor-like flourishes that Reed did on 86th Street. Raymond Avery simply measured and cut, as if he were cutting paper. At the same time, his eyes were alive in a deeper way than Reed's. Avery wasn't making conversation about the magazines on the table or about the Colts, but I felt he was paying more attention to me, in a more uncomfortable way, than Reed ever did. He was black, with handsome skin and a slight widow's peak he kept short and neat. I'd been working out for ten years, but I felt like a middle schooler next to him. He had the arms of a light heavyweight. He looked close to Isa's age. I decided, before I left the chair, that I didn't like him.

My dad started calling me around this time, in a way he never had before—often, and leaving messages—telling me about this canary yellow Chevy S-10 pickup truck that had come onto his lot. "I sold it, but the guy drove it home and his wife couldn't stand the color when it was parked in front of their house. He came back that afternoon and traded it in for another. The price point dropped four grand the minute it rolled off the lot, but it's perfectly good. Only a hundred thirty miles on it. Seriously. This is the deal of the year. I'll get you my employee discount and we'll start you building up your credit rating. You got the grown-up job; now you need the pickup truck."

"I don't need a pickup truck," I said. "What have I got to pick up? Everything I own came with the apartment."

"You're working now. You shouldn't be driving a Japanese soda pop can like you are. Get a man's car and see how it changes the timbre of your life."

"Changes the what?"

"Everything," my dad said. "Timbre's a brochure word,

college boy. Listen, you need a truck. How are you going to save the world in a Honda Civic? You can't even fit a good TV in the trunk."

"I can fit my TV in the back seat."

"I'm talking twelve thousand, two percent financing, building rock solid credit when you're twenty-three so you can maybe get yourself a decent mortgage one of these days. Plus, it'll look good on you, an S-10. Make you look a little sportier. Fun. You'll look like you don't mind getting a little mud on you while you're saving the world. But—and I know how important this is to you, son—they're still easy to park."

"I don't need a new car, Dad."

"It's still got rubber hair on the tires. Please, Brant, come look at it. Or someone else'll get it."

I had only been working at the prison for three months and already I felt suspicion moving beneath the surface of everything. My dad, I thought, had come to this: he needed to make his month's quota so badly, he was hitting me up. I knew he loved me and that this was probably what he thought of as a good deal, but I didn't need a new car and I told him so over and over, but finally, one Sunday two weeks later, I stopped by their house for dinner and saw the canary pickup in the driveway.

"Just look at it," my dad said.

My dad got on the phone after dinner, and my mother turned at the sink and said, "Brant, I hope you thanked your father for that ridiculous truck."

"What are you talking about? I'm buying it, aren't I? Now maybe I'll have this credit report he's always talking about and he'll get off my back."

"You act like you're doing him a favor. Are you telling me you believe that story about the color?"

"What?"

"That someone returned it because of the color?"

"That's what he said."

"Honey, your father is so proud of you. So proud. But if you think they're giving trucks like that away for half price because they've got a hundred and fifty miles on them, then you're not the boy I raised. You said last Easter you liked yellow cars, remember? Your father put ten thousand dollars down. It's a gift, honey. Your father just doesn't want you to feel like he doesn't respect you. He knows how proud you are."

When I was leaving that night, my father traded me the Chevy keys for my Civic and said he'd take care of the trade-in for me. I touched the Chevy's hood, which was still smooth and warm, the paint blemishless and bright. "Thanks, Dad."

"That's all right, son. You're doing good. This is my line, anyway. You can help me some day when I'm in prison."

"Right."

"We're proud of you," he said.

I climbed into the pickup, turned the key. My mother was at the kitchen window. I blinked at the glow of the unfamiliar dash. The window lowered dramatically. My dad was walking to the front door, waving but distracted, or acting distracted, by the rose trellis. I held a hand out the window and I waved good-bye and I felt like a cynical bastard, suspicious of everyone, and I didn't see what there was to be proud of about that.

Isa told me her car had cancer; it was leaking oil all over the parking lot. The engine light was constantly flickering beneath the speedometer. "Hot, hot, hot," she said, "but you know how it is when you're single: you can't take your car to a garage because then you can't get to work."

I told her I could pick her up on the way to work and she laughed. "That would get people talking."

"I don't care."

She flushed red. "Maybe I do."

That winter, her car did finally grind itself to death, and she had it towed to a service station. She asked me if I could give her a ride the rest of the week. "I took a cab today, but it's ridiculously expensive."

"No problem."

I dropped her off that afternoon. Her place was on the second floor of a generic apartment complex: a bunch of two story buildings with cheap iron railings. The narrow balconies were littered with old plants and dirty plastic chairs. It was one of those apartment complexes with a name like a Pepperidge Farm cookie—the Stratford, the Milano, the Chesapeake. I lived in an equally bleak place called the Nottingham.

Isa said, "There. With the red door," and pressed her fingertip against the cold windshield. It seemed like the end of a first date we hadn't gone on yet, which was awkward. The moment seemed to embarrass her, too; she was in a hurry to get the passenger door open. "You don't have to walk me up," she said. Then she stood on the sidewalk, leaning into the Chevy cab. I could see her breath. We agreed on seven o'clock the next morning. She said she'd be out at the curb if I called her a few minutes early.

"It's going to be cold this week. You sure you want to wait outside? I can ring the bell—"

"Don't be crazy. There's never been a man set foot in my apartment unless we both got drunk first."

"You'd rather wait in the cold?"

"I'd rather not clean for nothing," she said. "Good night."

Isa asked me to drop her off at the service station a few days later. "My car's ready," she said.

"Do you want me to go in with you?" I asked. "I know sometimes those places take advantage of single women."

Isa smiled. "I sure wish someone would."

"No. Really."

"That's nice. But you don't look like you know much about cars. Do you?"

"Not so much. My dad sells them."

"Well, these places don't treat college boys very well either. Now I know you're a man of the world, but I'm afraid it will be lost on them."

"Whatever."

"It was nice of you to offer," Isa said suddenly. "I mean, but don't worry about it. I've been getting by just fine on my own all these years. I can handle this."

"Okay." I heard myself mumble, "Thanks."

"For what?"

"I don't know."

"You're funny. Thank *you*. For the rides. I'll bake you some cookies."

I had a problem with a student. John Hill, a lean guy who constantly complained about the 200-word essays assigned in GED class, was cheating on a practice test, and got upset when I took his paper.

"I don't think that's fair," he said. He glanced at the men sitting around him.

"You don't think it's fair? That I caught you cheating and gave you a zero?"

"Man, you didn't even give me no warning! Whyn't you just pull me aside and say, 'Mr. Hill, you can't use your notes on this test.'"

"Did you see anyone else using notes?"

"I don't look at other people during a test. You'd probably think I was cheating."

"It looks to me like anyway your notes are just a line of multiple choice answers. AAABACBCDDACDBA. Since you want to talk about it, maybe you'd like to explain when in class you took these notes."

"Man, you didn't give me no warning. You should always give a warning."

"You don't need a warning."

"I got one now, don't I? A ZERO. Like I didn't get none of the rest of those questions right."

"Well, you can't cheat."

"This is bullshit, man. You treating me like a dog."

"Excuse me?"

"I said, this is bullshit. You always got to give a warning, man. You can't just be yanking a motherfucker's paper away."

"You need to watch your language."

"No other word for it. Bullshit."

"Mr. Hill, can you calm down?"

"I am calm. You're the one getting all hissy and tearing people's papers up and shit. For no reason."

I held up the paper in question. "Nobody's tearing—"

"Fuck this, anyway. I don't need this."

"You want to quit GED class, Mr. Hill? I can send you out right now."

"Do what you got to do, man. But I'll stay. I'll pass this test without you. Your *help*."

I told this story to Isa.

She listened intently. "You tossed his ass out, didn't you?"

I told her I'd let him stay. "I think he can pass the test."

"So who cares if he can pass the GED?"

"Uh, that's our job."

"No." Isa shook her head. "Not if he flunks the No-Test."

"The what?"

"The No-Test. You get a guy and he's all peaches and cream; he's your best friend. You don't even know why he's locked up here. Until one day you tell him NO, he can't do something—and then he goes all wet and nasty and a bunch of horseshit comes leaking out of his mouth."

"I'd hate for Hill to lose this opportunity just because of some petty shit in class."

"Yeah, well," Isa said. "It's his petty shit, not yours. Let him hate it. He's the one who brought the cheat sheet in. You deserve better than that."

"Are you feeling sorry for me?"

"Hell, no. We've all been there. When I started working, I had a clerk who taught me everything I needed to know about working here. Of course, that was by running every game in the book on me within the first two months. But I learned."

"His name Avery?"

Isa's eyes narrowed. "What did you say?"

"I asked if your clerk—if his name was Avery."

"I don't know what people told you. But yeah, his name was Avery."

Mr. Hill came into the classroom before the other students the next day and apologized. "I've got an anger management problem, but I'm in counseling for it. We got a group."

"That's all right," I said. "I understand."

He was pleasant and picked up the workbooks for me after class. "See you tomorrow, Teach."

"All right," I said. "Tomorrow."

As Isa, Liz, and I were leaving the building and Englehart was locking the doors, I mentioned John Hill's change of attitude. Isa laughed. "So he dogged you in class and apologized in private. I love it. And you lost a night's sleep over it, didn't you? Didn't you? You did. I can tell. You're like that. Oh well, I'm not going to give you any more advice about it, though I would have thrown his ass out. Or at least had him apologize in front of the world. Still, you should enjoy it while it lasts."

"What?"

"Being nice. Stick around, you won't be that way forever."

Englehart laughed.

The next morning, Isa and Liz came into my room while my students were working. All the khaki shoulders shifted when women walked up to my desk. Even the students who continued writing glanced up. "I wanted to apologize," Isa said. "Yesterday, I was a little inappropriate—I took a tone of condescension—and I shared your personal business in front of someone we work with. And I just want to say, today, that you are a better person than me and I'm sorry I got so sarcastic."

"Well, that's all right," I said.

"Sorry for disturbing," Isa said to the class.

The class watched the door close. A student by the window shook his head. "Miss Boone don't never apologize to nobody."

"She's in love."

"Enough," I said. "Get back to work. To *work*, people."

"What does condescension mean?" another student asked. "It gonna rain?"

That night wasn't Friday, but I asked Liz and Isa if they'd like to go to Heavy's with me. "Just for a drink or two." I found myself avoiding Isa's eyes.

"I can't," Liz Cady said. "Let me explain this to you: tonight is *Survivor*, and then *The Apprentice*. And then I have to go to bed, you see. That's how it works when you're over fifty."

"Sure, I'll go," Isa said. "Let's see how you drink on a Thursday for a change. I've got the feeling it's going to be interesting."

At Heavy's, I got out of my truck and saw Isa in the front seat of her car, fixing her makeup. It made me nervous. I was suddenly aware of the difference in our ages and afraid of how things were shifting, how we might not be just co-workers soon.

She saw me and smiled. Then she pointed me into the bar and held up her phone, opening it. Her mouth formed the words: "two minutes," and I nodded and went inside.

She joined me at a little table. I had ordered us a couple of Budweisers. When they were gone, Isa said to the bartender, "Why don't you give us a pitcher? And a couple cold glasses. I'm thinking that we're going to miss *Survivor* tonight."

"Who'd you have to call before? Can I ask?"

"A girl's gotta have her secrets. Not my boyfriend, if that's what you're thinking."

"What's your boyfriend like?'

Isa smiled. "Just ask me. I don't have one."

"Well." I raised my beer. "Here's to that."

"That usually works for me," she said.

As we drank, the table shrank between us. It seemed our elbows were touching more and our knees began nesting in between each other. I was aware of the heat of her face close to mine. I told her about my father, my truck, and about a truly embarrassing moment, which was getting turned down for the Peace Corps and how I hadn't told my dad.

"But isn't the Peace Corps really hard to get into?"

"Not really," I said. "You know that many people who want in?"

"I don't think I could do it."

"Well, I know I can't. They told me so."

"Don't think like that," Isa said. "What they really said was: I worked with Jack Kennedy and I knew Jack Kennedy and you're no Jack Kennedy. You're a mixed-up Hoosier kid with a secret prince inside and you can do more good wandering the earth in disguise, so go do it."

"They said they had no openings for someone with my background at the present time, but I should reapply in six months."

"And you said, fuck you, I'll go live my own life. I'll save the world without you."

"Yeah, I did," I said, "but not out loud."

"Say it. Loud."

I did. Isa smiled hugely, her chin balanced on her fist.

"God, I don't know anyone like you," she said.

"You surround yourself with sex offenders and drug dealers," I said.

"So do you."

"Well, it makes me the prettiest girl at the party," I said.

"Me too."

"And state employees have great benefits."

"There's that," Isa said, and she put her cell phone on the table in front of us. "As a matter of fact, let's call in sick tomorrow."

"Right now?"

"Might be a little tough after the next pitcher."

"Another?"

"Why not?"

"You're right. Why not?" I signaled the bartender. As I did, Isa picked up her phone and held it to her ear. She murmured to the prison switchboard operator, then left a message on the school machine. "You just called in?" I asked her.

"I might be busy later," she said. "What do you think?"

"Give me the phone," I said, "or do you think I should wait a little bit?"

Isa leaned over her elbows. "Don't wait. Anymore."

Isa turned on her living room light and dropped her purse. We undressed against the wall and found our way to her disheveled bedroom. I was on top of her and she told me to get a condom from her nightstand. I tugged the drawer open, reached in, found a gun. It was big and heavy, like a hammer. The only thing I could think was: somebody put a gun in your nightstand; who did this? I thought someone had broken into Isa's apartment and planted it there, like it was a TV show and she was being framed for murder. It was as if we weren't alone in the room anymore. There was a plastic box of bullets next to it, some empty rows visible in the honeycomb.

"What is this?"

"That's not for you," she said.

"Why do you own a pistol?"

Isa sat up, folded her elbows over her knees. "I'm a woman. I live alone. I work with sex offenders. You know, most of our guys, they'll be out within five years. It's not stupid. Actually, look at you: you might get yourself a gun too. Some of these guys probably got your number. Tell me you're not in the phone book at least."

"God," I said. "Is that the kind of world you live in? Where everyone you see every day—everyone you're trying to help—might be planning to get you someday?"

"I don't think of it like that."

"But you do." I put the pistol down on the nightstand, pushed the barrel towards the wall. "How do you stand it?"

She closed her eyes. "I can't think about it right now, all right? Let's not?"

"Okay."

"Is that all right?"

I looked at her body: the pale line of her neck, the newness of her breasts and stomach. "Yeah, that's fine," I said.

"Don't stop talking," she said. "I like your voice."

Her hands, my hands, were greedy. I found myself talking about something else, and I was glad to do so. "Me too," Isa said, over and over. "Yes."

I came out of the bedroom in the morning and found Isa in a T-shirt, eating breakfast without me. She stood at the kitchen sink, leaning over an orange bowl of cereal. There was a plastic carton of milk, a box of Peanut Butter Captain Crunch, and an open bag of Nestle chocolate chips. I saw her take a spoonful of the golden-chocolatey soup. She smiled and shrugged. "You caught me."

I watched her move awkwardly to the clean part of the counter. She pushed the cereal box to the edge, started to find me a bowl. I approached her from behind and wrapped my arms around her waist. Her ass was warm against me. She shivered nervously. There were dozens of questions I wanted to ask her, about herself, about who she talked to on her phone, about Raymond Avery. About myself and how she saw me. But I couldn't think of anything except that it's never impossible for some people to fuck up a good thing. I didn't want to be like that. I didn't want to expect the worst. I didn't want to be one of those people. And so I kept my mouth shut and was simply happy. Isa started to speak, and then she didn't. She just put the palms of her hands on my forearms and leaned back into me, tilting her face to meet mine, her eyes closed, lips apart. Happy.

THE GREAT ESCAPE

Isa said:

All the time I worked there I never heard of anyone trying to escape like in the movies, digging with spoons and
dropping sand out of their pants. I heard about two young
guys trying to climb the fence and getting shotgunned from
Tower #4. One of my co-workers was first on the scene and
described the steam coming out of the bodies.

For the most part the inmates live in dormitories, big
groups of fifty, and they have no privacy: windows onto the
toilets, bunk beds beneath fluorescent lights, no curtains or
coat racks to even cast a shadow in the room. Who is going
to dig? Even if no officer sees you on your hands and knees
in the dark, someone will tell on you.

But one guy did almost make it, now that I think about
it. He was from Kentucky and in my GED class. Never
said much. Wasn't a great student, and I wasn't even sure
he could pass the test. I could barely read his handwriting. He came to class and didn't complain, asked questions
every now and then. He had passed the pre-test and we had
ordered the real thing for him. He was all set to take it in

a week, which would have gotten him six months off his sentence if he'd passed.

But then we got a phone call from some woman in Kentucky saying she'd gotten a letter from this guy, her ex-husband, and he'd bragged about how he was going to pass the test and would be coming home early. "Hell if he is," the woman said. "I don't ever want to see that motherfucker again. You do know he got a GED here in Kentucky, don't you? In '94?" And she said the name of the adult education center where he'd briefly attended. It was true. He already had a GED.

So he was removed from the list, and we were sitting around thinking about how to write him up. Lying to staff, improper use of state property, none of it would do more than take away his commissary or give the guy some extra duty. There wasn't much sting to it. Then somebody said, "Hell, let's call it 'attempted escape,'" and so we did. That wasn't just a write-up; it was new charges, a new case being filed against him and he wound up getting five more years.

So no, to answer your question, I never heard of anyone escaping.

BILLY BECK:
He'll Only Break Your Heart

Billy Beck—six feet, three inches tall, wearing his usual oil-spattered camouflage pants and a sleeveless T-shirt, looked like a dirty tree standing in the brightest part of Nordstrom's. A woman leaning over the perfume counter bumped him and then checked her blouse for a sweat stain. Billy's thick shoulders and arms were covered in tattoos as elaborate as dollar bills. His skin depicted a samurai and a wingless dragon wrestling in a river, all of it inked green and red—and then, on his left arm, a chain of roses ending in the blue sunburst that covered the back of his fist.

Mike Pence, a thin thirty-year-old in a shirt the color of rice, came out from the back room and eyed Billy, who was helping himself to the demo bottle of Ralph Lauren Romance. Pence crossed the sales floor and tugged the bottle from Billy's wet hands.

"Honestly, Billy," he said, "can't you take a little care?"

"What do you mean? I care."

"You so do not care. Look at you! The way you're dressed! I mean: cargo pants? Sometimes I don't even know why you're gay."

Billy had what Pence referred to as "Fight Club" hair; it made his sudden laugh seem mischievous instead of rude. Billy pointed his chin at the bottle of Romance Pence was now holding. "I thought these were samples."

"And are you sampling cologne, or planning to wash your car? How much do you need?"

"A little more," Billy said, reaching.

Pence replaced the bottle on the counter and elbowed Billy's hand away. "Seriously," he said. "What can I do for you?"

"I'm on my way to Mexico and wanted to say good-bye."

"Are you serious? What are you talking about? You mean, good-*bye* good-bye? When are you coming back?"

"And I'm taking your car and your sister."

"My sister?" Pence exclaimed. Then his face changed. "She's driving the car home, isn't she?"

Billy nodded. He had his hands in his pockets, his forearms tightening as he rocked in place. "Probably."

"Chino?"

"He's out. He got released two months ago."

In the fluorescent center of the department store, the two men stared at each other. A mother and daughter shopping for cosmetics stopped, then walked around them. Pence suddenly threw his arms around Billy's neck. "Oh, I'll miss you," he said.

Billy nodded. "Yeah. Take care."

"Take care of my sister," Pence said. "Please. You know she's crazy about you."

Katie Pence, known as K.P., had a big Dennis-the-Menace smile and long dirty blonde hair that her brother described as "lemonade and rum." The homeless men downtown all remembered her slender, freckled body from the many times it walked by. She wore tight jeans and doll-sized T-shirts because she had a glass eye and didn't like people staring at it, or referring to her as "the girl with the glass eye." For this reason she also constantly carried an eighty-dollar pair of Ray-Bans, and she pushed these back on her nose as she leaned against the side of her car and waited for Billy Beck to come out of the Circle Center mall.

K.P. lived with her brother in their "ancestral home," a three-bedroom place that had been theirs since their mother developed Parkinson's. Irvington was a part of Indianapolis that had been known as up and coming for years, until real estate agents finally gave up on it. K.P. and her brother shared the house, both unwilling to sell it, and each found in the other a kind of practice spouse. K.P. had never had a serious boyfriend, which she attributed to her glass eye, while her brother over the years had gone through a series of men as if *boyfriends* were a magazine he subscribed to.

"What happened to Jason?" K.P. asked one weekend. "I liked him."

"Oh my dear," Pence had said. "Jason is so clearly a winter. And here it is, March. Time to move on."

Pence had never slept with Billy, though there was a polite level of flirtation in the way they teased each other. Truthfully, Pence was a little scared of Billy. He'd met Billy at the Old Point Tavern, where Billy worked. "Never date a bartender," Pence once whispered to K.P. "They don't really like people."

K.P. had felt differently about Billy since the day someone drove over her cat. Pence had come home after a frantic telephone call. He swiftly rolled up the sleeves of his Arrow shirt but then hesitated in the street, thinking maybe some kitchen gloves would be nice, and also a bucket. Basically he wasn't sure what to do, so he came back across the lawn to where K.P. was holding her wrist in the shade of the garage. "I need," Pence looked around the garage walls. "I better change clothes. We need a shovel, I guess." He was moving slowly, as if hoping a dogcatcher or the cat's friends or someone, anyone else, would arrive.

This was when Billy had shown up. His bicycle artfully dodged the pile of meat on the pavement and hissed to a stop in the driveway.

K.P. explained the problem. Billy looked at Pence. "Put that down. You're not going to bury him with a snow shovel. What's wrong with you?"

Pence shrugged. "I don't know. I don't have a lot of expertise in this kind of thing."

Billy nodded. "Hey, K.P. Go on inside. I'll take care of this." Billy gave K.P. a delicate hug and she shuddered against his chest. He passed her over to Pence, who ushered her into the kitchen and made her some tea.

K.P. thought Billy was tremendous for helping her, being such a "man" about it—and for accompanying them to the animal shelter a week later even though he was allergic to cats. She also thought that Billy had buried her old cat somewhere discreet—he'd hung the tags in the apple tree by the kitchen window. But Pence knew (because Billy told him later) that Billy had gone down the dead-end street until he found a car with blood and hair on a tire. He'd left the bloody cat on the seat behind the steering wheel.

"Very *Goodfellas* of you," Pence had said.

Billy shrugged. "I blame society."

One morning after that K.P. stood at the kitchen sink, drinking coffee and admiring the dreamy, mockingbird appeal of her cat's tags in the leaves of the apple tree. Her brother came into the room, and she turned and asked him, too casually, "Have you ever slept with Billy?"

"Me? No. Why?"

"He's like a deer trapped in the body of a Green Beret. Why can't sensitive guys be straight?"

"Billy's about as sensitive as a panther."

"Oh, you know he is."

"Listen, he's nice and he's not nice, okay? Let me tell you one thing about Billy: that is one gay man not at all in touch with his feminine side. The only reason he's not a Green Beret is he likes cock." Pence poured a cup of coffee, then put the coffee pot back and turned to his sister. "Do not get a crush on Billy. I'm telling you: he will only break your heart. I'm serious."

"Come on! I was just asking." K.P. laughed loudly and tossed the rest of her coffee into the sink.

When Billy came out of the Circle Center Mall reeking of Romance, K.P. turned the ignition. Billy suddenly filled the seat beside her. "What'd he say?" she asked.

"He reminded me that you're his sister and said if I sell you into a Mexican whorehouse I have to give him thirty percent."

"Just thirty?"

"He didn't start at thirty. I worked him down."

"Very funny."

Billy found his sunglasses and smiled. "No, he said not to break your heart."

K.P. grimaced at traffic, changed lanes. She didn't say anything.

Indianapolis darkened into a twilight zone of "Buy Here, Pay Here" used car lots and a crumbling Super K and a Target. They passed a house with painted windows that boasted tattoos, smoking paraphernalia, and "real newd girls"—and then Meridian Street bloomed again in the suburban sprawl of the Greenwood Mall. After the Bed, Bath and Beyond and the Panera, K.P. found Interstate 65. The world outside their windows slowly faded into cornfields and far-apart telephone lines.

"Did you know he was out?" K.P. asked. "Before this morning? Why's he in Mexico anyway?"

Billy pressed a fingertip to the windshield and spoke as if he were addressing someone on the horizon. "No, I haven't been in touch with him. I knew it was this year, if he didn't get any write-ups. And he's in Mexico because as soon as a Mexican does his time, immigration ships him back."

"Did you call him?"

"I tried," Billy said. "But it's his mother's number and my Spanish isn't all that good."

"She could put him on."

"She could," Billy said. "Except she's so glad to have her son back, she doesn't want anything to take him away again."

"Oh. It just seems a shame, since you waited for him."

"Not exactly."

"Maybe not exclusively," K.P. laughed. She pointed at his chest. "But in there."

"Yeah. Well. What am I going to say to his mom?" Billy made a fist over his knee. "No, *por favor*, I'm not a thug your son met in prison. I'm his gay white lover from three years ago. I doubt she wants to hear that about her baby. She's Mexican."

They did a McDonald's drive-thru after filling the gas tank north of Louisville. It was about six-thirty. They both got salads, though Billy didn't put dressing on his and ate it with his fingers while he drove. K.P. had apologized. "I can't drive at night," she said, motioning at her cheek and glass eye. "I have this depth perception thing."

"No problem," Billy said. "No problem."

A few miles later, he asked, "You can drive okay in the daylight?"

"It's worse at night."

"What happened to you? Your eye."

K.P. sighed. "I'll tell you sometime."

"Is it personal?"

"I just don't think it's the most interesting thing about me. But it's what people always ask."

Billy nodded. Louisville seemed to go on forever, like a state in itself. Billy commented that no one who wasn't from around Louisville even knew what "Kentuckiana" was. K.P. was surprised, though not particularly excited, to learn that the "tri-state area" didn't always mean Kentucky, Ohio, and Indiana. She was impressed, however, that Billy could speak about the East Coast from experience. He seemed to have been a lot of places—more than she would've guessed since he didn't own a car.

K.P. woke up when Billy pulled off the interstate. "It's okay," he said. "I'm just going to rest a little bit." He leaned over her to undo her seat belt. She leaned into his neck.

"Where are you going?" she asked. "Where are we?"

"Almost Memphis," he said. "It's three in the morning. It's a rest stop. I'm going to the pisser over there, and then I'm going to sleep."

K.P. watched him through the dirty windshield as he approached the bungalow of bright candy machines and toilets. She put her seat back, licked her lips, and tried to sleep. Then she opened her eyes, pulled the sun visor down and checked out her face in the mirror. She put on a baseball cap and tried to hide behind the bill.

In the morning, on the other side of Memphis, they managed to get to the river by parking beside a warehouse. Billy peeled back a broken section of chain-link fence. They came to a fishing spot where faded beer cans and cigarette butts choked in the mud. A flat barge slid past, dull and industrial, the water a thick and uninspiring color like bacon fat and chocolate milk beneath the sun. "So that's the Mississippi," K.P. said.

"How 'bout a swim?"

"Now? You're kidding."

Billy turned his head to survey the tangle of old grass and rusted fence behind them. The windowless warehouse crowned the hill. The air above its metal roof trembled in a heat mirage.

"No," he said. "I'm going in. Come on if you want to."

He tossed his T-shirt onto a patch of yellow grass. He sat beside it and levered his feet free from his Timberlands.

"You're going in," K.P. repeated.

Billy didn't say anything. He stood and pulled his jeans and boxers down. It was the first time K.P. had seen him completely naked, and she was struck by the sudden knowledge that part of him was pale and without tattoos. Billy stepped away, into the mud. "It's warm."

"Be careful," said K.P. "Is it fast?"

"It's okay next to the bank."

K.P. stood watching him. "You're a show-off," she said.

Billy Beck opened his hands to the sky, pulled down fistfuls of light, and grinned to the North, the South, the East, and the West. "I'm Huckleberry Finn all growed up."

"You certainly are." K.P. put her sunglasses on.

"You oughta come in." Billy backstroked away from the

bank. K.P. took a seat with her knees in front of her. When he repeated that she ought to come in, she just waved.

They walked back up the trail, Billy wearing his boots and jeans but dripping water from his hair. He'd used his T-shirt as a towel and now held it in one fist. "I love swimming," he said. "I taught Chino to swim, you know."

"I was there."

"Oh yeah," Billy said.

One Sunday morning Billy had brought Chino to the Pence house in Irvington. "He's never been in a private swimming pool," Billy said. "Only the public ones with a hundred other people."

"Well, *mi casa es tu casa*," Pence bowed with a flourish and waved them through the house. "It's still breakfast time for me. You need coffee?" Pence carried a coffeepot and the *Indianapolis Star* onto the patio.

Over the top of his newspaper, he watched Billy hold Chino up in the shallow end, their bath towels on a patio chair. Billy's tattoos took on a wet shine that made his arms look almost reptilian. Chino's real name was Orozco, but he washed dishes at the P.F. Chang's in Circle Center, and in the summer, with his deep suntan and narrowed eyes, his heavy crow-colored hair, he did look Chinese. He was maybe a hundred and forty pounds and all muscle—so much so that Pence, at thirty, felt overfed and middle-aged. Around eleven-thirty K.P. had come out of the house with her orange juice. It was the first time she'd met Billy;

he held one hand above his eyes and gave her bikini a thumbs-up.

"I'm Billy." He smiled and pointed his thumb at Pence. "You must be his sister."

"Yep. I'm K.P."

"You look great. Make me wish I was a lesbian."

K.P. laughed and waved to Chino. The Mexican didn't say anything. He didn't seem to blink. He looked over his shoulder. Then he smiled in a careless way at the house behind her. "Hey. How you doing?"

"This is the good one," K.P. said, pointing to her right eye.

In Tennessee K.P. bought a huge sack of Twizzlers at a Flying J truck stop. Billy scared her by making brown, unhealthy teeth out of some Tootsie Rolls. Whenever they stopped for gas, Billy did push-ups in the grass. When K.P. went inside a Shell station in Arkansas, the attendant said to her, "That boyfriend of yours really keeps himself in shape, don't he?" and K.P. felt the words in her stomach.

Chino had gotten vendor status in a drug case related to the apartment he shared with four cousins. "When could he sell it?" Billy had asked Pence. "I mean, he's got three jobs. He's working seventy hours a week. That little Aztec doesn't have time to be a drug dealer. Or else he just loves washing fucking dishes."

Billy went to visit him twice at Plainfield, the medium

security prison ten miles west of Indianapolis, and Chino sat with his arms crossed and legs splayed, like a sullen teenager. He refused to look Billy in the eye when they were in the visiting room.

"Stop looking at me like a faggot," Chino hissed.

"I am a faggot. You are too."

"Look," said Chino. "I'm the only Mexican here who's not a drunk driver or a drug dealer. I need friends, man. I don't need to be a fucking pillowbiter for these *cabrones*."

Billy had a bottle scar at the base of his neck from when he'd ejected two loud and heavy-elbowed Indianapolis Pacers from a bar (drunk, the two men had suddenly and loudly realized it was a gay bar). When Billy was angry, the scar stood out, bone-white, but at that moment it was just a pale seam in the center of his tattoos. He felt his lower lip trembling. He stared at the leather tennis shoes on Chino's feet.

"Fucking look," said Chino. "Look over there. You see that guy with the dreadlocks? That Cuban is doing twelve years for drugs. And he's smart, man. He's watching, man. He's always watching. People here see everything. Don't come visit me again, man. It's been good, but I got three years to do—and I don't really see how you can help me do 'em."

Billy tightened his face and watched the Cuban across the room. The broad-shouldered man leaned forward, elbows on his knees, and murmured to an overweight white woman. The Cuban looked up to see Billy's eyes, and Billy looked

away, his glance perfectly still and quiet. He had the prac-
ticed disinterest of a bartender as he surveyed the room. He
squared his eyes on Chino. "Okay," he said. "I'll write."

"Don't bother." Chino flattened his hands on his thighs
and pressed his khakis smooth. He made a vague, dissolving
gesture, then squeezed the arms of his chair. "I never went
to school. I can't read, man."

"You can read in the car?" K.P. asked. Billy nodded. He
had a biography of Tamerlane open against his leg. Beside
him, on the car seat, lay a thin paperback *Autobiography of
Benjamin Franklin*, a little Moleskine journal, and two Bic
pens he had rubber-banded together.

"I had no idea you were such a big reader," K.P. said.

Billy folded the biography around his tattooed hand. "You
read?"

K.P. shook her head. "Magazines."

"You're missing stuff like this," Billy indicated the book
beside him and started to tell her a story about Benjamin
Franklin.

K.P. interrupted him. "I don't miss it," she said.

Billy helped a trucker change a tire outside of Texarkana.
The trucker was very impressed with K.P.'s cut-off jeans.
"Those're some fine Daisy-Dukes you got there," he told her.

"Thank you," she said, and she crouched near the two
men and handed them tools. The trucker gave them a Tom

Clancy book, *Rainbow Six*, on eight CDs. K.P. was bored within half an hour, but Billy insisted on listening to it. "There are no women characters," she said emphatically. "Not one."

Billy gave her a blank face. "So?"

They got Subway sandwiches on the outskirts of Dallas, and as K.P. was unwrapping the cookies and arranging the Lay's, she asked, "What do you and Chino have in common, really? Besides the fact that you're both great looking?"

Billy made a courtly nod. "I'm thirty-two. Old for a gay man. Looks-wise, that's like fifty in heterosexual years. But thanks."

"Answer the question."

"You want 'things in common'? Really?"

"Yeah. Why not?"

"Why would I want to be with someone who was just like me? Do you want someone just like you?"

"Not just like."

"To laugh at all your jokes? I know people who are totally like that. They want a twin. Someone who thinks and acts like them. I think that's a bit narcissistic, myself."

"That's not what I mean."

"Or do you want someone who's been places you've never seen before? Who'll open the world up to you?"

"I don't think someone who speaks English is too much to ask for," K.P. said. "How do you know he feels the same way about you when you don't speak the same language?"

"Chino speaks English."

"I mean, really speaks English."

"I've got the English thing covered. Even big words. When it comes to a partner, that's not top on my list."

"Don't be so defensive."

Billy shook his head. "You just don't know him."

"I'm asking. I mean, I want to know him."

"When he said he loved me I believed him."

K.P. made a grimace. Then her eyes—her eye—rose up and met Billy's stare. "Tell me about it."

Billy set his sandwich back onto the unfolded wax paper and propped one knee against the dashboard. When he spoke again, it was to his knee. "When I held him, I felt his heart hitting me. Like a ram hitting a tree in his chest. And I didn't have to hold back with him. I could love him. All the way. You know what I mean?"

"I wish I did." K.P. looked out the window. In a quiet show of precision, she placed her sandwich back into a plastic bag. "I'm going to sleep for a while, okay?"

They crossed into Mexico at Matamoros. K.P. was driving. They saw huge lines—three miles on the odometer— of hot vehicles on the other side of the highway: smoking trucks and sunbright cars idling in the afternoon, making the sky wavy with exhaust, radios playing, waiting to get into the United States. "The war on terror." Billy's face was as blank as his sunglasses. "Do you feel safe?"

"No," said K.P. She nudged the car even faster. "I've never been to Mexico before."

Billy rubbed his unshaven jaw with the back of his hand. He set his stack of books onto the dash.

"No, no—I don't like the reflection." K.P. pointed.

"Sorry." Billy tossed the books onto the backseat. K.P. glanced over her shoulder at them and then back at the traffic.

"So just what do you and me have in common, exactly?" she asked. She tugged the wheel sideways. The car glided past a loud semi. The driver glanced down and Billy saluted him.

"Maybe nothing." Billy stretched, and K.P. could smell his sweat as his forearm hung in the air behind her. He studied her from behind his sunglasses. "Your brother," he said finally. "This car. Eating habits."

"That's it, huh? From what you say, we should be perfect for each other."

Billy laughed.

K.P. yawned and stretched her arms like Billy had done. Her shoulder pressed his bicep. "Why don't you drive for a while?" she said. "I want to look out the window."

Mexico had more blondes than K.P. was expecting. And the cars seemed the same. But then the omnipresent SUVs disappeared and the sky seemed to reach down farther, or maybe the buildings were just lower and farther apart. K.P. saw more and more window air conditioners, even on tall buildings, and then just open windows. She felt pale and graceless amid all the dark eyes of the people standing at street corners, carrying bags, watching the road from the shade.

Later in the day, the two stood barefoot at a gas station north of Ciudad Victoria, splitting two Coronas and some popsicles but not wandering too far from the car. "Tell me, what does he do? That makes you love him so," K.P. said. She glanced at her companion. They had been driving for hours, talking about other things—about how K.P. was thinking of going back and finishing her bachelor's, about how Billy liked working in a straight bar better than in a gay one—but when K.P. asked her question Billy nodded silently, as if he'd been thinking about that very thing the whole time.

"I can't explain," he said. "Chino can make me laugh, but he's not like you or me. He doesn't use irony. He's got no use for it. I don't know if it's all Mexicans or just him, but he—well, shit, he's not embarrassed by passion, you know?"

"I guess."

"I mean, in the States, I don't know—in the bar, every day, *The Bold and the Beautiful* comes on and we all watch it. But all the guys make fun of it."

"Because soaps are ridiculous."

"Well, maybe. Kind of. But the point is how uncomfortable people are—with a world where your feelings make you do crazy things and you don't give a goddamn."

"Sounds like a lot of drama," K.P. said. "I don't need that. I don't want to live a soap opera."

"No, I'm not saying it right. Forget I mentioned a soap opera. I mean an opera, period. Big voices in the dark. That's what I want. I mean, it's like I read once, John Gardner, pounding on a tabletop and telling his class, 'King Priam weeping over the body of Hector! That's literature! Everything else is BULLSHIT!' That's what I mean. Being with Chino, there were nights when I was pounding on the tabletop. I was fucking happy, man."

"I've never been to an opera," K.P. said.

"Neither have I." Billy had one foot on a stack of retread tires. His arms were crossed on his knee. He held half a popsicle and the last third of a Corona. His shirt was folded over his thigh and his skin was starting to sunburn so the green water of his tattooed river looked stained with blood.

"I can't explain it—wouldn't even talk about it if I wasn't so nervous."

K.P. threw her popsicle stick into an empty oil barrel. "Let's get going," she said.

"Good idea." Billy bit off the rest of the popsicle and drank his beer over it.

After dark they stopped at a drugstore that was so bright they could see it from four miles away, even when they were on the neon street it faced. The store seemed to have a ceiling composed entirely of fluorescent lights. Billy went in to buy some amphetamines Chino had told him about; he wanted to drive all night and make it to Mexico City the next day. There were teenagers smoking cigarettes out front, and K.P. didn't feel entirely secure sitting in the car. When an old man with a California Angels cap pulled over his afro pushed a shopping cart up against the bumper of the car and knuckled the window six inches from K.P.'s face, she made frantic signs to show she didn't speak Spanish. Then she started the car. The old man seemed alarmed at this and started pulling on the door handle, but with the engine on, the doors had locked. He started hitting the window with the palm of his hand. K.P. pointed a finger at him, shouting: "Get the fuck off my car!" and that was when Billy came out.

The man seemed to sense Billy approaching him and turned in place. Four teenage boys and their girlfriends started shouting, and someone threw some potato chips at Billy and the old man both. Billy reached into his plastic bag and put the package of amphetamines into his pants pocket. Then he handed the old man a Snickers bar. The man almost dropped it, as if he hadn't used his hands for that purpose in a long time. He started to shuffle off as Billy passed him—but suddenly Billy stopped with one fist trembling in the air, his body cocked like a gun. The old man cringed, folded up, raised his elbows. Billy said something in Spanish and pointed at K.P. The man hung his head, then wiped his palms on his pants and held one hand out. His eyes were the yellow color of the moon. Billy stood for a moment, glaring like a heavyweight boxer, but then he reached out and shook the wrinkled hand. The teenagers clapped and one of the girls started to sing the Spanish "Amazing Grace," which made Billy laugh and stare at the ground, then look up at them and then the stars and then the man again. K.P. had her window down now and she heard Billy's last words to the man: "*No, tú estás viejo. Yo estoy stupido. Muy, muy, stupido.*" They exchanged smiles and Billy opened the car door and K.P. slid over so he could sit.

A block away, K.P. said, "I thought you spoke Spanish."

"Sure, I speak it," Billy said. "I speak it like a small child."

K.P. wanted to talk about every detail—What did the guy want? Was he mad at her? Was he hungry?—until Billy interrupted: "Jesus, who the hell cares? You think it's right to scare the hell out of a woman in a parking lot?"

"No, no, it's not."

"Scaring old people's not too cool either," Billy admitted, "but old people shouldn't fuck up."

He drove a couple of blocks. As they waited for a light to change, he said, "You ought to know by now. I'm a fucking bully."

They got to Mexico City late, dead tired, Billy driving. "We've got to find a hotel," K.P. said. "You need a shave."

Billy pulled into the parking lot of a bank. K.P. had a map unfolded across her lap and Billy thumbed through his black journal. He read her an address but she had to see it herself. "*Calle mayor . . .*" Because the worldwide supply of pay phones was dwindling, they couldn't find a set of yellow pages. They had to find Calle mayor and then drive in circles until they found a hotel. "I know we can stay there," Billy said, pointing through the windshield.

"Why?" K.P. had her window down and one arm out, looking.

"Because it says Holiday Inn. You see it?"

"Oh, yeah." K.P. leaned back. "How 'bout somewhere else, okay? I know you're tired and it's totally retarded of me, but I can't stay in a Holiday Inn with you—I just can't."

"They're really not that bad." Billy massaged the steering wheel.

"Please."

"Okay."

K.P. rolled up her window. "The first time I ever spent the night with a boy—not the first time I had sex, okay, but the first time I spent the night—it was at a Holiday Inn. After the prom my senior year."

Billy grinned. "Oh, really?"

"I was with this guy, Hartwell, who was like the biggest jock in school—but smart too. Good looking. He went to Notre Dame in the end. You'd have loved him. But he was so not gay. Believe me. I was in love with him from junior high on. He never paid me any attention until about a month before the prom. He asked me. We started going out. The night of the prom, we double-dated with a friend of his and this girl Mandy I kind of knew. Hartwell and I had only gone out maybe three times. We did have sex the weekend before."

"You slut."

"Yeah, I know. I was going to save myself for prom, but . . ." K.P. gestured dramatically. "Anyway, Hartwell and his friend got us adjoining rooms at the Holiday Inn. So we went to dinner and the dance, and then we went to the hotel. We had the doors open and had a party. Until finally we shut the door and the other couple were in their room and we were in ours."

"And you got sick."

"No, I can handle my liquor. I don't know what kind of girls you're used to. No, I was drunk but not bad. Hartwell drank more than me. We fucked. It was all right. It was good for high school if you know what I mean. And that was the first time I'd ever had a big bed and a night to fall asleep in. He taught me what spooning was. I'd always thought it was something dirty. But we fell asleep holding hands."

Billy glanced at the headlights in the rearview mirror. They threw a rectangle of light across his eyes. "That sounds okay."

"Except I heard voices. Around three in the morning. You know what he was doing? That prick? He and his friend had opened the door. He had his friend in there and they were checking me out. I honestly think they were getting ready for a trade. I'm not kidding. They were going to switch places. I woke up and wondered where the sheets were, and then I felt them standing there in the dark."

"What'd you do?"

"What do you think?" K.P. made an ugly face.

Billy nodded. He didn't say anything, but he drove with his left hand and his right hand found hers on the seat. He squeezed it lightly. "We all been there," he said. "One way or another."

They found a room in a tiny, non-chain hotel about two miles from Chino's mother's street. They both took showers. "That's so good," K.P. said. "I'm ready for another already."

The room was the size of an American guest room, with a little knee space around the double bed and a new air conditioner installed in the window. The television was suspended from the ceiling on a steel shelf that looked like a trapeze. The old woman who owned the building had given them a stack of white towels, none of which unfolded to be larger than an American hand towel. Billy had been sitting on the edge of the bed, holding his forehead as K.P. got ready for her shower, so she said, "If you want to shave or something, go ahead. I guess I don't have to be shy around you at this point." So he'd stood at the tiny sink while she showered and steam spilled out of the refrigerator-sized bathroom. K.P. slid the shower door open and held a series of the white towels to her skin. Billy squeezed past and took her place as she clambered out and made wet footprints beside her dufflebag.

That night Billy dressed himself in his usual Timberlands, but with clean, almost dark blue, jeans and a white shirt with pearl buttons that hid his tattoos, except for the ones beneath his collar. K.P., who wasn't going to meet anybody special, put on a clean pair of jeans, some sandals, and a Gap T-shirt.

They found the apartment building where Chino's mother had always lived. Billy had the address in his journal. "The first floor here is our second floor," murmured Billy. "So I'm thinking it's that window there. The fifth one up. You see that clothesline? I know that dress, yeah. Chino sent it to his mother for Christmas. Your brother helped him pick it out."

K.P. didn't say anything, so Billy squinted at the pavement, then the window, then back again. "I'm going up."

"You want a wingman?"

"No, no—I'll meet you at the hotel."

"Maybe I should stay away from the hotel for a while."

Billy flashed his smile. "You think you can go to the movies for a bit?"

"Sure." K.P. looked up and down the busy street. "I'll find something to do."

"I don't even know if he's home."

"Someone will be."

"Maybe he's . . ." Billy let the sentence trail off. "Thanks, K.P. Thanks for everything."

He kissed her on the cheek. K.P. found herself holding her palms in the air, afraid to touch him. She was aware of his face and his smell—no Ralph Lauren now, just his unfamiliar man-scent. He backed away from her. "I'll see you back at the hotel in two hours. Tell you how it went. He's probably not even home."

K.P. watched Billy cross the street. She started for the car, but turned to stare at the glass door of the apartment building. They had driven almost two thousand miles and Billy didn't even know if Chino was home. He hadn't seen him for three years. This was the soap opera life he wanted. K.P. started walking for the car. At the corner she stopped in a market and bought a Coke Light, which tasted odd but good. She watched the apartment door and saw Billy and a smaller, mustached man come through it. Chino had gotten wrinkles around his eyes, was not so boyish anymore. Beside them was a thick-necked version of Chino, maybe an older brother. Billy tried to slide a hand onto Chino's shoulder, but the smaller man brushed it off.

An hour later Billy called her at the hotel and asked her to meet them for drinks. They'd already had a few. Billy introduced her to Chino's brother as "my girlfriend, K.P." Chino smiled, pinched her elbow, and asked how she was doing, what was new in "India-nap-police." K.P. sat at one side of the table as the three men spoke Spanish. Eventually the brother got up to leave. Chino pulled him back down. This happened twice and K.P. was exhausted, ready to sleep herself, ready to make excuses somehow and just say good-night, but then the big brother did leave, telling the bartender nevertheless to send another round to the table. Billy seemed to be buying. Once the brother was gone, Billy watched Chino without blinking and Chino got up to use the bathroom.

"What's going on?" K.P. asked.

"I don't know," Billy said, but his voice was angry.

"Don't talk to me like I'm a child," K.P. said. "You called me out here and now no one's talking to me."

"Not you, too." Billy rubbed his head. "Look, I don't know what the hell is going on."

Chino came back with the three beers his brother had ordered. "K.P.," Billy said, "you want to leave us alone for a little bit?"

"No, I think she should stay," said Chino.

Billy folded his arms, his biceps swelling around his fists. "Why?"

K.P. nodded. "Yeah, why?"

"Because," Chino said, "we call her out in the middle of the night. She was tired, maybe, a long day. And we got three beers. She's your girlfriend, right?" Chino raised one beer, but no one clinked it.

"I was just telling her about how you didn't do that," Billy said.

"Do what?"

"Use irony. Say things you don't fucking mean. You used to just say what was in your heart."

"Three years a long time, man." Chino gave his bottle a quarter turn.

"Is that it?"

"Part of it, yeah."

"Say the rest."

"What you want me to say, Billy?" Chino flattened a hand on the table. His nostrils widened. "Why you showing up now at my mother's house? My family, they don't know about me, man."

Billy didn't move. His eyes were blue and cold. "Sorry."

Chino took a drink and set his bottle down with a loud smack on the table. "I'm moving to Minnesota, man. My cousin is working there. Going to get me on the floor at a mountain bike factory. Start this over."

Billy didn't say a word. Chino started talking to K.P. "What he doesn't understand—we were good together, but it's like that happened to somebody else. Three years is a long time."

"You have no idea," Billy said.

"Oh yeah, I do," Chino said. "You gonna make me say it, Billy? All right, man: we're through. Until you showed up at my mother's house, I'd forgotten all about you. I jack off about you sometimes, but that's it. The moment's gone. I'm never going back to Indiana."

"You could have called me from Minnesota," Billy said.

"Maybe I would've."

"Don't bother now." Billy got up, threw some money on the table.

"Hey," Chino said to Billy's back. "Who asked you to come down here, man? Who are you mad at?"

Billy had stopped moving for as long as Chino was talking, but a moment later went out the door. K.P. started after him. Chino pressed his fingertips against her arm. "You don't have to go," Chino said. "Let him cool off."

"You disgust me," K.P. said, shaking her elbow. Chino let go.

She followed Billy out the front door. He bristled with hot menace. The tattoos on his neck seemed thin and tight. His jaw was hard. A tall Mexican approached, talking into a cell phone. His elbow hit Billy on the shoulder. Instead of stepping away, Billy closed in—so his chest pressed against the stranger. The man stumbled back, mouth open, trying to speak. Billy's blue eyes flashed and the man raised his phone, as if to hide behind it. "Sorry," Billy said. Billy's fists emptied, fingers pointing to the ground, shaking slightly. The man hurried off, talking to his invisible companion and glancing backward. Billy watched. K.P. caught up to him and put one hand on his shoulder and another at his elbow. "I'm okay," he said. "I'm okay."

"I know it," she said. "Let's just walk a bit."

Their clothes smelled of cigarette smoke. Instead of taking a cab, they walked all the way back to the hotel. K.P. held Billy's arm at first. Then they walked side by side. Near the hotel, an old man was selling cans of Heineken from a Styrofoam cooler. He was drinking one himself. Billy and K.P. bought one each. They drank their beers in the hotel room because they were too tired to walk anymore. Billy turned a chair toward the window and pretended to be interested in the dull glow of the city rooftops. He stared at nothing, with the air conditioner blowing behind him. K.P. took her beer into the bathroom and closed the door, got into the shower. She stood there for a while, drinking beer, feeling the hot water, until she was ready to pass out. She turned off the light and found that Billy had turned out the bedroom light and was already in bed.

In the dark, K.P. laid her towel over a chair. She elbowed her way into an extra-large T-shirt and tiptoed into some underwear. Billy lay on his side, staring at the pale crack between the curtains. She lifted the covers and discovered he was naked except for his boxers. "I don't have pajamas," he murmured. "Does it bother you?"

"No," she said. "I wear less than that. When I'm not on the side of the highway."

Billy shifted and looked over his shoulder, forced a smile. "You're in a bed now," he said.

K.P. felt her face heat up. "No."

Billy's voice was humorless. "Don't want to tempt me?"

"Don't."

"What?"

"Don't make fun of me."

"I'm not." They lay apart, Billy with one fist beneath his pillow and one beneath his jaw. K.P. lay on her back but watched him.

"I just want to hold you," she said.

"All right." He raised one hand, reached blindly for her behind him. She rolled over and slipped one arm under his, and he pulled her chest against him, pressed her hand flat between his chest and his palm. Billy let her spoon her long legs against his and she let out a gentle breath. "Thank you," she whispered.

He pulled her hand down to his cock, which filled her hand but didn't move. It was warm and lifeless. "Nothing is going to happen," he said. "I'm gay. Do you understand?"

"Yes." K.P. found herself blinking something back. "I understand."

"Okay."

K.P. nodded. Her hand cradled his sex and she said, "Think about him."

Billy closed his eyes. "That's all I've been doing."

"It's okay. Tell me about him. What you liked."

"I can't. No. He's not worth it."

"Shh."

Billy didn't say anything. K.P. rubbed her chin against his shoulder.

"Three years ago," she said, "when you brought him to our place for the pool?"

"There's so much more to him than you saw tonight," Billy said. "I don t know why he was acting like that."

"Just think it . . ." K.P. sat up and leaned over Billy's waist. With her free hand, she pulled the covers back. Billy turned to face her, but she pushed him towards the crack in the curtains. "Just think about it," she said.

Billy closed his eyes. His cock was expanding in her fist. He remembered a night when he and Chino both smelled like cigarettes. When he'd felt eight feet tall, and he'd had Chino's unfamiliar body in his single bed. Then he felt K.P.'s mouth: a delicate, nestlike warmth that he grew into.

"K.P. Don't."

K.P. let go of him long enough to say, "Shhh."

"K.P."

"Stop, Billy."

"What?"

"I want to be him. Let me be him. Please."

"Okay," Billy said. "Stop talking."

Afterward Billy cooled and moved away from her in the bed. K.P. pulled off her T-shirt and emptied her mouth into it.

"Thanks," Billy said. He couldn't look at her legs or the pale triangle of her underwear. He glanced at her bare shoulders. Her hands. The wall. "Do you want me, I don't know, to do something for you?"

"No. Let's just go to sleep."

"I'm sorry."

"Don't be. You made me happy."

"It's not right."

"Stop talking," K.P. said. Then she tugged him by one shoulder and pulled herself onto him. "No, there is something you can do. Look at me. Look me in the eyes. Please."

Billy fixed his gaze on her. His eyes didn't blink. It was almost the disinterested look he used in the bar, but not quite. K.P. stared back at him for long seconds. Then she started to cry. "Thank you," she said.

"We're a fine couple," Billy said.

"But we are," whispered K.P. "We are. We are."

THINKING LIKE A COCKROACH

When Englehart was OJT (on-the-job training), Sergeant "Brutus" Harlan told him that if any inmate gave him any bullshit, to just write the guy up, no questions asked.

ENGLEHART: Okay.

HARLAN: What's more, you see a guy out of place, write him up.

If he smells like he's been smoking, write him up.

Any little thing, write him up.

ENGLEHART: But I could just—I don't know. That seems a little harsh.

HARLAN: Criminal thinking is like a cockroach, see?

ENGLEHART: No.

HARLAN: Roaches mostly come out at night.

You feel me?

ENGLEHART: Yeah.

HARLAN: You see one, you know there are hundreds around.

You can't let yourself think that the first time you caught the guy was the first time he ever did it.

What would the chances be?
The very first time a man decides to buy
some grass, he gets arrested?
You believe that?
Nah, it ain't like that.
Here, in prison, no, anywhere, for that mat-
ter, you see someone doing something,
you know he's doing it behind your back.
You know he did it a dozen times before you
caught him.
It's not the first time he's pulled that shit.

ENGLEHART: But you could say the opposite, too,
couldn't you?
About good behavior?

HARLAN: What?

ENGLEHART: That for every good thing you see someone do, they do more when you're not
around?

HARLAN: Nah.
No. Not really.
You can fake being nice.
You can't fake being shitty.

OVERHEARD:
Officer Winston, Officer Englehart,
and Sergeant Harlan

WINSTON: Harlan? That's a bitter man.

ENGLEHART: No, no, he's not. He's all right.

WINSTON: Ask him what he hates. What he hates most
              in the world.

ENGLEHART: Why?

WINSTON: Go on. Ask him.

ENGLEHART: Hey. Harlan. What do you hate most in
              the world?

HARLAN: How many things can I say?

ENGLEHART: Oh. How many?

WINSTON: Tell him three.

ENGLEHART: Three.

HARLAN: I hate old people. Yeah. Because they smell
              and they can't drive. And little noisy kids.
              I hate them, too. Because they're so noisy.
              Okay, and I hate women who cry. Ah,
              fuck it; what other kind are there? I hate
              women. I really do. Old people. Children.

Women. That's three things. Any more
stupid fucking questions?

ENGLEHART: No. Just checking.

HARLAN: Japanese pickup trucks too, if you're interested. I'd have said Jap pickups, if you'd
given me four choices.

ENGLEHART: That's okay.

HARLAN: I hate you too.

ENGELHART: Excuse me?

HARLAN: If you'd have given me five, I'd have said
you.

WINSTON: All right, Harlan.

HARLAN: But I just met you. You can still make the
top three if you stay here long enough.

BRANT GILMOUR AND ISA BOONE:
Part 2

I liked the gym. I had been too self-conscious to even think about trying out for a team in high school, and I couldn't watch pro sports without thinking about the excessively pretty grass and the toxically bright uniforms or the hulking kidney danger of all the obvious steroid use. And the commercials! The car ads made me feel like I was trapped on the phone with my father. But I liked doing push-ups and dumbbell curls and jumping rope in a gym.

I liked the gym because it was a place where I felt alive. I liked to see my mirrored self floating upward beneath a pull-up bar. I liked to listen to my shoes hitting a tread-mill. I felt like a character in a movie. I'd been small as a child, always the last one picked for games. In high school, I'd used my dateless evenings to run. In college, when my classmates were giving up sports for beer and internships, I'd started lifting weights and felt good about it all. I'd see a guy in a movie leap from a roof onto a moving car or climb up a rocky cliffside, and I'd think: I could do that. It made me feel, in one small way, that maybe I'd grown up to be the person I'd always wanted to be.

Prison is not like the movies, where every inmate lives on the weight pile and their muscles are tied to more muscles until prison uniforms look like overinflated balloons. Plainfield, at least, was not like that. Many of the offenders were loud-talking, underfed, would-be gunslingers who didn't have any muscle beyond what was necessary to wave a pistol around a room. Or they might be hollow-faced scarecrows who'd sacrificed their teeth and body weight to crystal meth. Or they were middle-aged sex offenders who only preyed on people naturally smaller than themselves. Of course, there were inmates with cannonballs for biceps and footballs for calves, and some middle-aged inmates filled their shirts like they were young men, but a lot of the guys I met were in prison because they were lazy and I was bigger and stronger than them.

Isa didn't get it, my morning workout thing, but on the weekends she'd go eat breakfast and meet me afterward. This Saturday she'd been to Starbucks and was doing something on her cell phone in the foyer of the Y when I came out of the locker room. She continued squinting at her phone as I opened the door to the parking lot. "You have a good workout?" she asked.

"Yeah," I said. "How are you?"

"Great," she said. She held up three fingers. "Three cups of coffee. A little sugar and milk. My insides are a furnace. If I worked out, I'd be unbearable."

"You think? Unbearable?"

"I'd be so smug, you couldn't stand me. Everyone who works out is unbearable. But people who work out first thing in the morning are the worst."

"Hey, what are you saying?"

"You're impossible," Isa said, "but you have moments of decency. I saw that girl in there looking at you."

"Who?"

"Barbie. With the red T-shirt."

I looked back through window. "Her? She works there. She looks at everyone. That's her job."

"She takes her job very seriously."

"I don't even know her name."

"It's Pence," Isa said. "She's employee of the week. I heard all about it while I was sitting there. Her and her friends, blah, blah, blah. How do you stand it?"

"You want me to get fat?" I asked her.

"Am I fat?" she asked.

"No. You're all right. But if I don't work out—"

"You'll probably whale up to one seventy. Brant, right now I weigh as much as you."

"No, you don't. I'm one fifty."

"I'm one thirty-three."

"No."

"I am," Isa said. "You're fooled because of my delicate bone structure. From the belt up."

"You look good."

"Brant, you are so full of it. Anyone can tell: you've got the body of a rock star. I look like I've had two kids. Your wallet makes you look fat. If I were your height, I'd kick your ass, easy."

"You couldn't do it," I said. "As soon as we started to wrestle, you'd take your clothes off."

"You'd take my clothes off."

"I would."

"Well, we'd fuck like monkeys. And since you always fall asleep after, I'd win."

"So when you said kick my ass, you meant a T.K.O.?"

I stole a glance to see if she knew what T.K.O. meant, and it was clear from her happy smirk that she did. I'd had girlfriends before. But my main college girlfriend had always been seeing someone else. She called it "dating," but a friend of mine who knew her from high school called it "slutty" before I told him I wasn't interested in his opinion. She and I had broken up before Christmas of my senior year. I'd been fixated on Pearl when I graduated, but mainly because she seemed unobtainable, like a painting I could never carry out of the gallery. No girl had ever treated me like someone she'd be excited to tell her friends about. I was always kissed experimentally, as though my biggest appeal was that I was still under warranty.

Isa's ass filled the passenger seat, and her giant purse was like a picnic basket on her lap. She tapped her phone against the palm of her hand and I spied on those delicate hands and her intelligent eyes and the way her chest made small but lovely curves in her tank top. She smelled like a big city or something expensive, like perfume, and not a college girl at all.

BRANT GILMOUR AND
JOHNNY WALKER WINSTON

The prison functions with a Conduct Adjustment Board that screens the offender write-ups and issues penalties such as loss of recreation or loss of commissary or loss of earned credit time, which means an inmate will be released later. In an effort to make the process more impartial, the board rotated membership, with a lieutenant representing custody and then, usually, another officer or two, but ideally someone from non-uniformed staff too. When I was in my second month, the supervisor of education sent me down to represent the school. "It'll be good for you," he said. "You'll see how the rest of the camp operates."

The C.A.B. met in the maximum security wing, but only because the guys in segregation usually had write-ups and were a pain to move around camp. I found Lieutenant Sharkey sitting at a desk. Some tattered Garfield comic strips were taped to the file cabinet behind him, and a marine corps emblem held a position of honor beside the padlock bar that clamped the cabinet shut. Lieutenant Sharkey was a lean blond without clear eyes and a twitchy chin. He seemed to be composed of pure animal mean, but, after looking me over he offered me some coffee and showed me where to sit. "You mind filling out the paperwork?" he asked. "That'll make things go faster."

"If you can read my handwriting, I don't mind."

"Christ, another one of those. Teachers! You went to I.U., didn't you?"

"Yeah."

"I'm a Purdue man. But that's all right. No one'll get hurt. We got Johnny Walker coming."

"I didn't even say yes to coffee."

"Ha! That's his name. You'll like him. He's up in Tower #4."

A few minutes later I was shaking hands with an officer named Johnny Walker Winston ("Tell him how you got your nickname, Winston" "Later," he said), who was my dad's age but with a kind of Robert Mitchum face. He loosened his Sam Browne belt as he took his wooden seat.

The first case we heard was a guy who'd refused a direct order to take a shower. He was a foul-smelling man, maybe three hundred pounds of sweaty deadweight. I had no doubt that his T-shirt, unwashed to the point of resembling coffee with a little bit of milk, was probably another two pounds of solid stink.

"You plead guilty, right?" Lieutenant Sharkey said.

"Not guilty."

"Not guilty?" Sharkey said. "I know you haven't taken a shower in at least two weeks; I could smell you when you walked in the room. Matter of fact, I think we're going to have to repaint in here now, you son of a bitch. What do you think, dumb ass? You think we're fucking stupid?"

"Officer's got no business telling me what to do with my own body. He just want to see me naked."

"Man, no one wants to see your fat ass naked. A starving fucking tiger wouldn't want to see your fat ass naked. You know Doctor Phil? You get Oprah in your dorm?"

"Yeah."

"Well, this ain't about you! You're a fucking health hazard for the rest of your cube! People can't eat around you. Now we're not going to take your recreation because obviously you never go to the gym. But we're going to take your commissary privileges for a month, and if I get a call from—" Sharkey stopped when Winston touched his arm.

Winston addressed the inmate. "Why don't you leave the room while we confer?"

The inmate got up and went out the door.

"Shut it," Sharkey shouted. Then he turned to me. "That's my bad. We're supposed to confer about whether he's guilty or not."

"Oh, I think he's guilty."

"Aw, no question. He's obviously guilty," Sharkey said. "Y'all think a month without commissary is fair?"

"Give him time to run out of Honey-Buns and soda," Winston said. "Be good for him."

"Come on back," Sharkey yelled. The inmate returned. "We've considered your statement and find you guilty of refusing a direct order, a 355 C write-up. We're restricting your commissary privileges for thirty days, starting today. And I'm telling you, personally—what dorm are you in? 14-North? If I get a call from Larry Wiseman down there tonight and he says you aren't clean enough to fit through a basketball hoop, I'm coming down there with E-squad and we're going to cuff you up and hit you with the fire hose. You understand?"

"I get it, I get it," the man said, and he signed his paper and left.

"Send the next guilty bastard in," Sharkey said to the door. Winston smiled but shook his head, and Sharkey turned to me again. "See, this is what's great about Winston. He makes sure the process works."

"Yeah, I see that. But if he's the good cop and you're the bad cop, what am I?"

Winston turned in his seat. "That's an interesting question. What the hell good are you?"

"Even his handwriting sucks."

"What good are you, son?"

"I can spell," I said, and I pointed to the form Sharkey had just filled out. "Hygiene doesn't have a 'j' in it."

Winston put his hand on my shoulder. "Get this boy some coffee," he said to Sharkey. "He's going to make it just fine here."

"Here, you son of a bitch." Sharkey grinned. He passed over his clipboard and ballpoint. "I don't care if you do have pig-handed handwriting. You're doing this from now on."

We saw eight more cases that day. Three innocent, five guilty. Some of the write-ups were hard to read because a lot of the officers only had what I would guess was an eighth-grade reading level.

In one case, a four-hundred-pound, bearded white guy was accused of ferrying drugs around the camp in his wheelchair. It had a special seat made for really big people and the stitching had been torn in such a way that things could be hidden inside. Things had been hidden in worse and more foul-smelling places. "What's wrong with your legs?" Sharkey asked. "Can you stand up?"

"Not really," the man said. "It's not my legs. It's my kidneys. I'm on dialysis and I've got chronic diabetes. The write-up says I'm making deliveries. Honestly, sir, if I could get up and down that easy, I wouldn't be in this chair. I have a pusher from the porter's room, a different one every day. If I were making deliveries, I'd have to cut him in on it too, and I'd have no way of knowing who I was getting and I'd have so many partners it wouldn't be worth my while. That officer in dorm 13 just don't like me for some reason. I don't know why."

"Will you step out a moment while we confer?" Sharkey said. I got up and wheeled the man into the hall. Sharkey tapped his pen on the clipboard. "What do you think? He's making sense to me."

"He could trade porters," Winston said. "And he's not FedEx. He could hold his deliveries for when he got his man. What's his handicapping condition, except basically he's fat and abused drugs? I say guilty."

"Being fat doesn't mean he's guilty."

"Well, okay, there's this. Guys on the sidewalk don't think I can hear them up in Tower #4, but I hear a lot when I got the window open. 'Bout a month ago, I'm watching this guy on the walk. He tells his porter to slow down. Basically, he wants to watch the basketball game behind dorm 13. I never seen him slow down before, but that day a bunch of the young ones are playing with their shirts off. If he ain't a chickenhawk, I don't know who is. Ten to one he's here on a molesting charge. And then, to top it off, you know what I hear him say?"

"What?"

"He complains to his porter about all the niggers ruining the NBA. Says that with all the niggers in the bloodlines, America's gone to hell. The guy's a four-hundred-pound child molester who can't walk a hundred yards and he thinks he's part of the master race. He sits there in front of us and I can't believe a word he says. If he says it's hot, I'm getting my jacket. If he says he's innocent, I'll bet you my lunch he's dropping dope all over this camp."

"Sounds good to me," Sharkey said. "Guilty. How 'bout you, Teach?"

"Sure," I said. "Let's get him done and then send the next guilty bastard in."

"I love this guy," Sharkey said. "Get in here!" he shouted at the door. "Gilmour, see if your boss'll send you next week."

JOHNNY WINSTON:
All Along the Watchtower

Johnny Winston had spent fifty summers mostly outdoors and had the red-brown neck and forearms of a farmer. His eye sockets were pale from his sunglasses. Johnny Winston was like a lot of the officers at Plainfield Correctional Facility; he couldn't touch his toes or run a mile, but he could easily and "accidentally" slam a door on a man's fingers. Self-defense, it was said, started the second you thought something bad might happen. Johnny Winston was hard as he had to be, though it gave him no joy, really. He had worked road crew for the county and he'd run a press at the Daimler-Chrysler plant before coming to Plainfield. At the Chrysler plant, people called him Johnny Walker because of one particular softball game he'd pitched. He'd been known for his sense of humor. At the prison, he sometimes missed being known as funny.

His favorite joke, before he came to Plainfield, went like this: An explorer is in the Amazon looking for cannibals, but then he finds some and all his party is killed. The guy is left running through the forest with an entire village behind him. Arrows are going through the trees like in Indiana

Jones. The guy runs through the jungle, but suddenly the leaves give way to a clearing beside a river. There's absolutely nothing to hide behind. He runs out onto a sandbar and about a hundred cannibals come out of the woods, spears in their hands. He's staring at them. There's a giant waterfall behind him, and the guy drops to his knees and cries out, "Oh God, I'm so fucked!"

But then a voice, a deep and warm and powerful voice, answers him: "No, my son. Look down. There is a pointed rock beside your knee. It's just the size of your hand. In a moment the chief will approach you. You can pick up that rock, rise to your feet, and strike him between the eyes. He will not raise a hand against you."

The man looks down and sees the rock. Then he looks up and, sure enough, one giant cannibal has stepped forward from the rest. He's got feathers hanging from his hair and red paint up his arms and chest. Everyone gives him space as he walks out onto the sandbar carrying a giant knife. The explorer picks up the rock and stands. The chief comes forward so his chest is almost touching the explorer. The explorer can smell the chief's breath. He lifts the rock into the air and swings it down. Crack. He nails the Indian right in the face. The chief falls into the water and goes over the falls. For a second it's completely quiet. Then every single Indian at the edge of the river starts to scream. "Now," the voice from above says, "Now you're fucked."

Winston worked the dormitories for three years, and that was, he thought, the worst job possible. Supervising men as they did nothing. It was day after day, night after night, of telling one man to put a shirt on and another to pick up the dirty toilet paper he was using for Kleenex. It was catching men having sex in the toilets. Writing men up for playing tag like children. It was listening to a grown man beg to change beds because he owed another man Hostess Ho-Hos or soap. It was scolding young kids who fought over nothing or who refused laundry call-out and wore the same stinking T-shirts for days. Even at night, when the offenders were supposed to be asleep, there was always someone out of area. Some noise. A closet door to check. Men running around barefoot, giggling—or at best, just lying there and farting, a room full of unhealthy men passing gas and coughing in the dark. There were two officers in each dorm, maybe a hundred and fifty inmates, and it made the time go by slowly, day and night, the volume on every conversation just a little too loud because of the echoing concrete floors.

After three years in the dorms, Johnny Winston had gotten a work line and run the yard crew. It put him in charge of twelve offenders instead of a hundred, but he got tired of being out in the snow when the walks needed to be cleared, of squinting into the sun to watch the fluorescent safety vests near the road. Years before, an inmate had run off from a work crew and they'd had to get dogs and shotguns out and chase him down. Winston wanted nothing like that on his watch. Then one spring an offender drove a lawnmower over a piece of exposed sewer pipe and sent a metal shank into the door of the superintendent's car. Winston found himself assigned to the kitchen. Sergeant Connolly repeated Winston's old joke back to him, the one about the cannibals.

"You remember how you didn't like working the yard in the middle of summer? How you didn't like standing around with inmates and snow shovels, five a.m. New Year's Day? You thought that was the worst job in the camp—you did, didn't you?"

Winston nodded.

"Well, now you're fucked," the sergeant said.

It was about thirty degrees hotter in the kitchen than in the rest of the camp. He was constantly counting everything, trying to stop the trafficking in stolen sandwiches, in extra oranges dropped onto trays, in double scoops of pudding. He had to write all that up and though it had its comical moments he still hated it. He got tired of repeating the story about how he caught an inmate with eighty-two frozen burritos in his coat. The sugar and yeast were padlocked in cabinets because they might be used to make liquor. And there were always the knives and can lids and other sharps and class A tools he had to keep track of, the big forks and the hot surfaces someone could get a face pressed to. It was a stressful job, and it was a wonder anyone could survive four years there, but he did.

When the officer in West Tower #4 retired, Johnny Winston bid for the post. He had sixteen years in with the state, so he got it. Up in the tower he sat in a cushioned metal chair and watched the yard and the fence. That was it. All those noisy inmates—that giant bus station of homeless people yelling at each other—they all turned into khaki fish floating from one side of the grass-colored aquarium to the other. The brick buildings went from dim to dull in the midday sun, then back to dim. The sidewalks did the same. The offenders marched back and forth in long lines—the brown pants and T-shirts walking from dorm to chow hall. To the chapel. Back again. The blue pants, new to the place, walked so much slower in their own lines. The yellow pants stood outside the health unit, waiting for an officer to open a door. Sometimes yellow pants actually climbed into vans and went through the gate—to some hospital where they'd be handcuffed to a bed, then returned like a package a few hours later.

Winston never felt the need to sneak magazines into his post. He wasn't a big reader. He listened to the prison radio traffic and was glad he didn't have to run anywhere when a fight broke out. Glad he didn't have anybody to count at count time. He could hardly explain his happiness to anyone, not even to his wife, who'd known him through almost every job he'd ever had.

A few years before, two twenty year-olds had actually been shot off the fence. They'd made a run for it right beneath the South Tower where Betty Gaston had been posted. She was fifty-eight and like a grandma for some of the inmates. Betty was one of the nicest people around the camp and everyone knew that. The two kids who got shot had figured she wouldn't shoot them if they weren't hurting anybody, just trying to get home to their families. They leaped onto the fence and started climbing. One of them had a coat inside another coat, and he tossed this over the barbwire at the top. It wasn't clear how they'd get past the second fence, but it didn't really matter because Betty Gaston leaned out of South Tower #6 and shot the first boy straight down, so the shotgun pellets went through his face and one shoulder and some were found in his stomach. The other boy hit the ground like he'd been shot too, but he hadn't been. He'd just shit his pants and lived. He got another seven years for attempted escape. Betty Gaston took a few weeks of stress leave. Then, not long after she came back, she retired. She was named employee of the year, which might have seemed a little tasteless, but everyone who worked at the facility understood. Except for a few of the young new guys, no one wanted to be Betty Gaston.

Johnny Winston hadn't seen her in ten years. Now that he had a tower of his own, he liked to imagine he was the only person who'd ever sat in it. He didn't particularly enjoy the winter. The wind came right through the frames of the plexiglass windows, and it was like being a lifeguard at a cold and empty beach, sitting in the high chair and shivering. Sometimes his friend Harlan would spy on the silhouette in the tower windows, and as soon as Winston ducked into the little toilet, Harlan would hit the radio and make him come out. "Hey, who's watching these guys while you got your pants down at your knees?" But that was all part of the job. Winston clocked in, got a shotgun, rode the truck out to his post, said good-bye to whoever was driving that day, then climbed the metal spiral staircase to the top.

After that, he said to his wife, it was like fishing. He watched the day go by, and from up there it was all gentle and reassuring somehow. All the stolen burritos and the un-Biblical sex, all the hidden cigarettes and infected tattoos, the chaos—everything seemed peaceful and calm, like ripples on a lake. He had never seen anyone make a break for it—and because of Betty Gaston, he didn't think he ever would.

BRANT GILMOUR AND ISA BOONE:
Part 3

Liz Cady's clerk was a well-behaved child molester. ("They make the best clerks," she whispered, "but not the best tutors because the young black guys won't sit near them.") Her clerk was just supposed to keep the file cabinets straight and grade math worksheets, but he also seemed to grade spelling papers and, really, as far as I could tell, everything else, too. He tabulated little "report cards" for each student every week while Liz sat with her elbows on her desk and pulled fun-size Three Musketeers bars from the top drawer. "You should get a clerk," Liz told me. "I know Isa doesn't like them, but it is such a time-saver."

"What is she saving time for?" Isa asked me when I told her. "Have you ever seen Liz Cady at the blackboard?"

"She teaches some."

"I'm not saying you have to be a *Little House on the Prairie* schoolteacher, doing chalk-and-talk at the front of the room, but a teacher should be up and about. Know students' names. That kind of thing. The only time Liz gets out from behind her desk is carpet time."

"Carpet time" was Isa's name for Liz's favorite end-of-class activity, which was having her guys pull chairs into a circle so she could read aloud from a chapter book. It was an exercise that, for Isa and me, balanced equal portions of narcissism and stupidity.

"Is she just showing off?" I said. Isa and I were in the hallway, backs to the wall beside the open doorway. Liz was breathlessly recounting the story of some orphans who were having an apparently very exciting adventure completely lacking any sex, drugs, or violence. The men were blinking at her. One had his head on his forearm, asleep.

"They're grown men," Isa hissed. "They're forty years old and haven't learned to read yet. Why does she think they're going to learn by hearing her read *The Boxcar Children* out loud?"

"Well, they're listening to a woman talk," I said. "Thirty minutes without interrupting. That's good, don't you think?"

"You are such a girl," Isa said. "You kill me. Do you get your bullshit off Oprah or do you make it up yourself?"

This is the way we talked; I drove a Ford pick-up truck and did 200 push-ups a day, but, according to Isa, she was more manly than me. She never went so far as to say she wore the pants (and I wore the Dockers), but that was essentially the joke. One day in class, John Hill—my unhappiest student—decided he wanted to know what kind of car I drove. He kept proposing different cars. ("You drive a Jap car, don't you? You got a Civic?) When I shook my head, he kept offering other makes ("You got one of those Korean knock-offs.

A KIA.") until I said that he didn't need to worry about it because it wouldn't be on the GED. He laughed that off and suggested I drove my parents' mini-van, which led me to tell him we were done talking about my car. He shrugged, raised his hands and eyebrows—and then proceeded to talk about a woman he knew named Jesse James.

Wanting to talk about my car didn't seem to merit a formal conduct board, but I was at a loss as to what else I might do. I didn't do anything. When I told Isa about it, she said, "Oh, don't worry about it."

"I just feel like no one in class today learned much that would help them pass the GED. They learned what a comedian John Hill is. And about how his girlfriend takes pole-dancing classes."

"These guys have had ten or twenty years to learn what most people learn in junior high. If you didn't make the most of one hour or two, it's okay."

"I guess."

"You're so sensitive. Don't be such a little girl. Don't bring any of their B.S. home with you. None of them matters," Isa said. "Brant, you need a little less Dorothy in you and a little more Scarlett O'Hara."

As a rule, I only spent the night at Isa's place if we were both quite drunk or got carried away. She said she preferred my apartment in downtown Indianapolis even though it lacked blinds or curtains and the previous tenant's cigarette habit had given my ceiling a carmelized look. If Isa and I watched a movie or got take-out, it was usually at my place, but she rarely spent the night. "I won't do the walk of shame down that hallway in the morning," she said. "Your neighbors are scary enough when I've got a beer in me."

My place was half an hour from her place in Plainfield and forty minutes from the prison. That was probably part of the appeal for her. I got the feeling that Isa didn't want to pack lunches or drive to work together in the morning. There was the whole secret-from-our-co-workers thing—but also her often expressed fear that I might get too good a look at her in the morning, as if her sleeping face without makeup might make me reconsider everything. One night I woke to find her getting dressed. Her quiet smile was like a present she was giving herself. It filled her face in a clumsy and unfamiliar way. I wasn't used to seeing her smile unless it was at something funny.

"See you, Cinderella," I said. She rushed back to kiss my cheek and push my shoulders back into the pillow.

"See you tomorrow," she said. She pushed my hand away from the light switch.

I got up and stood at my curtainless window and watched her drive away, then went back to bed and waited until it was light enough to call her.

Another night Isa and I were parked at the curb in her Pepperidge Farm apartment complex. The shadowy metal carports and the poorly painted shingles and uncut hedges gave everything a lurid Halloween look. We'd been out to eat, and Chick-fil-A wasn't exactly romantic, but we'd sat for two hours just talking like a couple of teenagers, first over meals and then milkshakes. It seemed like we would never run out of things to talk about—her sister, her parents, her life, mine—and she loved my yellow truck, loved to put her bare feet on the seat beside her, said it made her feel rich to ride in a new car like that, and it didn't seem like she was older than me. We just told stories to each other. She never gave me advice except mockingly. She never acted like she knew more about teaching than me. She should have, really, because I was often quite lost.

That night in front of her apartment, I wound up with my hand in her jeans, so much so that she whimpered, "My underpants are soaked. Get your hand out of me." But she didn't reach for my arm. Her palms were flat against the seat. We were both sweating and I whispered, "Who's the girl now?"

"I am," she said. "I am. Let's go upstairs." And I followed her out of the truck as she struggled with her keys and opened her front door and then we fell on each other on the living room floor, beside a pile of her old shoes and a stack of yellowing newspapers. When I got up, I realized that we'd shut the screen but not the front door. Isa laughed. "Don't let it hit you on the way out."

Isa was a terrible housekeeper. She had piles of laundry she referred to as spring and summer. The third time I spent the night at her place, I said, "I think we need to wash these sheets."

"I just changed them," Isa said.

"When?"

"That first night."

I discovered that she had cleaned her room in a violent and rapid way the first night I'd come in. She'd stalled me in the hallway with the "need a second" ploy then thrown her dirty clothes and magazines and spray bottles from the carpet to the center of the bed and tied the bedclothes into a bundle and changed the sheets. When I found the bundle in the closet, I said I'd wash it all for her as a birthday present. "Don't hate me," she said.

I was at the laundromat when I opened it. Only one other person was there, which was good, but this was a pretty young woman about my age who had been halfway glancing at me over her *Runner's World* magazine and her iPod. Then I opened the bundle and half a dozen *Marie Claire* and *Us* magazines, Windex, a bottle of hair spray, some jeans, underwear, a dozen T-shirts, and a giant rubber sausage fell out of the sheets and tumbled to the dusty and hair-covered tile floor. The last item I didn't recognize because I'd never owned a dildo personally. I held it up in honest curiosity. My neighbor in the laundromat burst out laughing and then waved her hands at me.

"You just look so mortified," she said, pulling one of her earbuds free. "I'm sorry."

"Well," I said, "this is certainly the last time I do my grandmother's laundry."

I returned the laundry, folded in my basket, to Isa's. I left it in front of her door with the magazines stacked on top and the dildo in a ziplock bag.

She called me when she got home. "Thanks a lot. I'm sure my neighbors are glad to know I'm not alone. That was a nice touch, bagging Mr. Handsome up like evidence."

"Mr. Who?"

"Mr. Handsome. That's what I call my helper. Since now you know everything about me."

"I'm not surprised you know your assailant by name. In most sexual assaults, the victim knows her attacker."

"Brant," Isa said. "What Mr. Handsome does to me is not rape. I guess you'll never understand the bond between us."

"I don't want to. I'm afraid Mr. Handsome would treat me like a cub scout. He seems—"

"Listen to you," Isa said. "I was talking about my feelings. Come over tomorrow night, pervert. I'll buy you a pizza."

One afternoon Isa put one shoulder in the doorway of my classroom and shook her head side to side. "Look at you," she said. "It's ten after three."

"We don't get off until three-thirty."

"Why do you think we send students back at three?"

"So we can lock everything up. Get ready for tomorrow."

"Yes," Isa said. She sauntered in, took the stack of math

workbooks from my hands, and slid them onto a random shelf. "And because it takes fifteen minutes to get from here to the parking lot."

"Englehart told me that at Marion County jail, it takes half an hour just to get out of the building. When the fire alarm goes off, they just move inmates from one floor to another."

"Fascinating," Isa said. "All I know is I'm not going to be behind that fence for thirty seconds if they're not paying me."

"I need to grade these worksheets before tomorrow."

"If you even try to bring those home, I swear to God, I will break your arms."

"When do you do your grading?"

"What do you mean? I do it right in front of them. I make them watch me and see what they're doing wrong."

"With every guy?"

"I find the threat of real embarrassment can motivate even the laziest motherfucker."

Dennis Herbert had been locked up almost as long as I had been alive. He was the kind of person who'd be invisible in a group of ten or more, but as soon as you noticed him in the back, you'd squint and try to figure out what was wrong with him. In the prison, where the offenders wore identical khaki shirts and elastic waistband pants, Herbert was a bit like Mr. Toad in *The Wind in the Willows*. His clothes seemed hugely expressive through their chaos. The wrinkles in his shirts were like giant fingerprints. Half his name was magic-markered across the shoulders of his coat, but apparently his pen had run out of ink.

I tried to give him a nickname. I called him Secret Herbert and Spices around the other teachers. They all thought it was clever, but too long. Herbert's skin was freckled with age and the color of brownies. He brushed down a thin rub of ashlike middle-aged hair, and his giant, thick glasses made his face seem like an approaching alien spacecraft. He had a way of speaking that was a mixture of the professorial and the liquor-impaired. "Mmm, well, you see," he would quietly rumble, and then stare at you without another word. It was hard to say if he was joking or not.

He was working in maintenance when I met him. A lot of inmates had inside-the-fence jobs like that. They made about 70 cents a day. Herbert spent mornings pushing a wide dust mop up and down the hallway of the school. One Monday morning about eight o'clock, he was leaned against the radiator and I said, "Man, this week is really dragging on, isn't it?" He chuckled. We stood there in silence another minute, and then I asked him if it was Miller Time yet.

Herbert started talking to the empty hallway. "Mmm, well. You see, one time I had this uncle. who drank Miller High Life. The Champagne of Beers? He worked in the Chrysler plant near Oakland City. The whole shift used to keep Styrofoam coolers in the trunks of their cars and when they got off, they'd meet in the parking lot and drink a Miller High Life. Or two. Sometimes they'd go to some-one's house or a bar, but mostly they'd just drive home after-ward. One night my uncle hit a man who was walking on the side of the road. A country road. Dark. So he stopped and he got the guy up and into the car, drove him thirty minutes to the nearest hospital. And the guy winds up suing him for $150,000. My uncle has to work an extra ten years, until he's seventy-two. Right before he died, we were at a softball tournament and I was getting some lawn chairs from the trunk of his car and there was a Styrofoam cooler in there, along with a brand-new shovel. 'What's the shovel for?' I asked. 'That's in case I hit someone on the way home,' he said. 'I'm just going to bury the motherfucker.'"

Herbert mumbled this story into the empty space between the ceiling and the far wall. He stood against the radiator, his hands behind his back, and rocked his ass against the metal as he talked. When he was done he wandered down the hall and started picking up paper from the tiled floor and carrying it to the trash.

I decided around that time that I'd like to hire Mr. Herbert to be my clerk.

One afternoon I watched Herbert unfold a torn length of clear plastic. "I see you got yourself a prison briefcase," I said. "That for your legal work?"

He smiled quietly. "Well, you see, Mister Brant, it looks like rain out there. So this old plastic bag, it's my raincoat, you understand?"

"Don't call me Mister Brant. You make me feel like we're on a plantation."

"My people's from Mississippi," Herbert said. "That's how we talk."

"Mister Herbert." I stepped forward. "My name's Gilmour. Not Mister Brant." He and I shook hands—which was technically against the rules.

"Mister Gilmour," he said. He started to leave the room. "Mister Brant? None of my business. But remind me to tell you the two most powerful words in the world sometime. Because I like you."

"One of them start with 'F' and other one 'you'?"

Herbert chuckled. "Not even close."

"You're going to teach me your secret words? What if I get all your powers?"

"No secret to my powers. Just no one can do what I do." He walked out of the room, plastic bag around his shoulders, like a homeless Santa Claus. His right hand reached up slowly to tilt his giant glasses back on his face. Neither one of his heels rose more than an inch from the ground as he noiselessly made his way down the hall.

The next day I said to Herbert, "How about those two most powerful words in the world?"

"Well," he said, "for this to make sense you have to realize that only about ten percent of the time people open their mouths, it's to give you information. Or to ask for some. The other ninety-nine percent is just to say, Look at me! Look at me!"

"Who taught you math?" I said.

"I got my GED at this here institution. You saying I didn't get a good edumacation?"

"You're right." I said.

"I right a hundred-ten percent of the time. But it ain't nothing to be bragging on." He smiled. "The other fifty percent I'm full of shit. But you a big boy. You already figure that out."

"The two words?" I said.

"Well, timing is everything," Herbert said, "and to be honest, I don't think the time is ripe for telling you just yet."

One afternoon when Liz was doing special education paperwork, she sent all her students back to the dorm but borrowed Herbert from building maintenance so he could get her iced tea from the kitchen and staple her paperwork. I didn't see how he could work for Liz Cady. He seemed like he could see through her fat white woman friendliness to all the bullshit inside, and he seemed unstable enough to say something about it. But it wasn't the first time Liz Cady had press-ganged him into helping when her usual clerk wasn't there and when I walked by, he seemed content at his little desk. At one point Liz had to step down the hall to the bathroom and left Herbert alone with the special ed folders. This was technically illegal, but the arcane paperwork inside was of no visible interest to Dennis Herbert, and the fact that many of our students were low IQ or learning disabled wasn't exactly a secret. Still, as she passed my room she asked me to keep an eye on him. I was on my prep period.

"Mr. Herbert," I said. I waved a hand at the papers arranged like Bingo cards in front of him. "How do you like your new job?"

"Well, you see, I been doing it two hours now and I see it's kind of like a marriage," Herbert said.

I gave him a look. I didn't like the implication about Liz Cady.

"I just mean that I'm always wrong," Herbert said.

"Come with me for a second, would you?" I locked the door behind us and opened my own classroom. "You give me a hand cleaning this place up?"

Herbert squinted around the room. "Well, certainly."

"Just clap the erasers somewhere out of sight. By the dumpsters. And sweep up the floor. That would be great."

"No problem. I can do that."

"You ever want a regular classroom job? Grade papers, sit in a desk, deliver some stuff up and down the hall? Instead of pushing a broom all day?"

Herbert looked around. "The desk have a drawer?"

"Let's not get carried away. But you could use my pens to grade with. And if you wrote a few letters for yourself on the side, I wouldn't care."

"You couldn't give me a pen to keep? Miss Cady, she give her clerk a set of pens."

"Hey, to me, that's trafficking, and I like my job."

"You're somethin' else, Mr. Brant. An ink pen? You can't let go an ink pen?"

"You want to be a clerk?"

"Let me think about it. I'll think about it," Herbert said, stacking the blackboard erasers. I got back to work but casually watched him clean. Before he left, he gathered up a pile of *Sports Illustrated*s I'd stacked by the trash. I knew he wasn't going to the dumpster because he'd already been.

"How are you going to get those past the officer at the front?" I asked. "He's going to write you up for theft."

"I'll say you gave them to me."

"I'll say you're lying. You're welcome to them; they're two months old. But if I gave them to you, that would be trafficking." I smiled because Herbert was grinning at the floor. "I just threw them away. And you're on your way past Sergeant Brutus and his all-seeing sunglasses."

"He do see a lot," Herbert said. "He don't see everything."

"I don't imagine he does."

"But he do like to write," Herbert said, referring to the endless stack of conduct reports Brutus famously completed on anyone in his area. "He maybe thinks Oprah's going to have him on her show."

"Her book club?"

"Yeah." He busied himself with his coat. "When I was at the prison in Michigan City, up by Chicago, we'd see Oprah's plane go by overhead."

"How can you tell it was hers?"

"It say OPRAH on it."

Herbert sauntered away from me, nowhere to go really but sensing that was his exit line. I waved good-bye, and he nodded. I saw Herbert approach Sergeant Brutus at the offi-

cer's cubicle. They had a few words, but not loud or unpleasant ones, and Herbert sauntered away, hands in his pockets,
and I knew the old black man was carrying a hundred pages
of old magazines somewhere behind his wrinkled coat, but
I couldn't see where. Brutus saw me staring down the hall
and he looked around, then cocked a finger like a pistol and
pointed it my way. His thumb went down and I dodged
slowly behind the edge of my doorframe, and looked at the
clock, ready to go home.

The inmates called Sergeant Harlan "Brutus" because he
had a thick beard that made his lips and chin invisible, His
belly forced his belt buckle down in such a way no one could
see it either. Harlan was probably the only person within the
fence who didn't think he resembled the Popeye character.
He liked to joke around, but if he thought for a second people were laughing at him he would make them miserable. I
saw him write up a number of black guys for having their
trousers too low. "If I wanted to see your ass, I'd talk to your
pimp," he said. One day he found a piece of sharpened scrap
metal between the pages of an auto body textbook—it was
clearly a shank—and he started a campaign against students
taking books in or out of the school building. "I can't check
everyone's books—there are two hundred students. What's
more important? Safety and security, or this guy studying
something he should be learning in class anyway?"

"How can we run a school with no books?" I asked him.
"No homework."

"Maybe it will take a guy a little longer to get his GED. So what? They've got time. What's the rush? Isn't that better than having people getting stabbed on the walk or in the dorm. Or here in the school? You want to get shanked?"

"No," I said.

"Brant won't get shanked," Isa said. "He's too pretty."

"That's true. That's true," Brutus said. "He'll be a hostage. Like you, Miss Boone. Me, I'll get shanked."

I looked at Isa. Brutus was swaying with happiness, rocking on his heels. He seemed proud of the notion that inmates would kill him if given the chance.

"If someone wanted to kill me," I said, "he could keep a shank in his sleeve or pants long enough to walk up on me. He wouldn't need a GED book."

"You think you could handle being a hostage?" Brutus asked Isa. He seemed to be staring at her mouth. "They wouldn't let you go."

"Brant will protect me," Isa said, which forced Brutus to glance my direction.

"Yeah, right," he said. He started to say something else, but I held up the palm of my right hand and turned it so the blade was facing him.

"Sergeant," I said, "I could put this through a half inch of particle board. Pull a man's throat through a buttonhole in his shirt."

"Ha," Brutus said, but he rocked back on his heels and then sauntered away. "See you two."

"You're so full of shit," Isa said to me later.

"Particle board makes me so mad," I said.

"As if you could punch through it."

"Did I say that? I didn't know what I was saying. I thought we were going to fight over you."

"You better win," Isa said. "Holy shit, you better. That guy gives me the creeps."

"Don't we all?"

"Him more than most," Isa said, "and I work here."

Herbert came to my room not long after that and said he was ready to enlist.

"Enlist in what?"

"Your assistant."

"Well, now," I said. "Today, that depends. Today, there's a test. What are the two most powerful words in the world? Open Sesame?"

"I never understood that," Herbert said. "What was that supposed to open again?"

"Ali Baba's cave."

"Who's Ali Baba?"

I made a V-sign for two. "Two? Words?"

"You sure you old enough? I hate to pass on the forbiddin' knowledge to you if ain't old enough to use it—what we say? Wisely."

"Mr. Herbert?"

"Mmm?"

"Are you telling me that you don't want to tell me two magic words you learned because you're afraid—me, look at me—I may use them for evil? Not good?"

Herbert laughed. "All kinds of evil in this world."

"That's true."

"You might use them on Miss Isa."

I frowned. I never let an inmate discuss my personal life. Or the female staff.

"I say that because I use them a bit in my work for Miss Cady. Nothing bad. But here's the words. You ready?"

I nodded vaguely.

"The words are okey and dokey."

I stared at him. "That's it?"

"That's it?" Herbert mimicked my voice in a way I'd never heard him talk before. In two words, he made me sound like William F. Buckley. Like I was 300 pounds of white. "Them two words is everything I know on this earth, Mr. Brant."

"I don't get it."

"What I've found is that nothing brings on bad times like saying NO to the Man. But if you say, 'Sure, boss,' then he'll keep on walking and you can go on back to doing what you're doing. And if he catches you later? That's when you say, 'Oh sorry, boss, thanks for pointing that out! Guess I misunderstood.' That's all you need. You say, 'Okay, sorry, boss,' and you do it his way for a little while, 'til he forget about it and then you go on back to doing it your way. He don't want to do your job too. So he ain't gonna stand there and watch you do whatever it was he said. Matter of fact, he won't even remember what it was in a month. But you say NO? To his face? Well, shit, it's over. He'll be all on top of you like sauce on spaghetti. It's over."

"I can't believe I just gave you a job," I said.

"But look at me. I'm being honest with you. You catch me not cleaning your erasers or whatever—none of this shit is too hard—you fire me. I ain't going to fight about it. I'm giving you advice for life here. This could change your life."

"This advice might be worth a little more if you weren't in prison," I said.

"That's true," Herbert said. "You a smart one, Mr. Brant."

I shrugged dramatically.

"Anyway, okey-dokey, those are two powerful words. But I guess, they're not the—what you call—the motto of my life."

"Which is?"

Herbert wiped his fingertips on his shirt. "*Too little, too late*. But you got a chance. You young."

I told this to Isa while we were eating Taco Bell at her apartment. She grimaced. "You ought to fire him. I get that he's funny, but shit, do you really need someone to grade your spelling tests? He's not that special. He thinks he's smart. He'll talk up one day and you'll fire him. You wait and see. You just better hope that happens before you catch him stealing. Or selling your tests."

"Well, I know you don't like clerks."

Isa stared at me. "You don't know shit."

"I'm asking."

"You're fishing. I'll tell you the whole story, Brant. You want to know? You want to know if I sucked his dick?"

"No, no. I know you didn't do that."

"You know that?"

"Yeah."

Isa seemed to be thinking. She crossed her arms. "You've been working at Plainfield—no, you've been working, period—how long? Eight months?"

"What's your point?"

"You really don't know anything about people yet."

"What, did you? You went down on that guy? Your clerk?"

Isa hissed. "Get the fuck out of here, Brant."

I stared at my food for a second. It was a congealed and comfortless mess. "I'm out of here."

"You're such a prick."

"Whatever."

"Grow up."

"Be like you?" I said. "Smug and condescending? Is that what you mean?"

"Who's smug now?"

"Fine," I said. "I'll call you later. I think we need some time apart."

"You think?"

"I'll call you."

"Yippee. I'll be right here. Like this." She held her phone between her breasts as if it were a baby. I left and heard the phone hit the door behind me.

The next time I saw Isa, she didn't speak to me. She looked at me like I was sculpted out of horse feces. I stepped into her classroom at lunchtime and she rose to walk me to the door, saying we didn't need to talk because she didn't have anything she needed to say.

"Well, maybe I do," I said.

"Maybe you do. But you're not saying it."

"I just want—" And as I said this, Isa slammed her classroom door on me. I reached out, like a fool. My fingers must have made a sound like balloons popping because I felt my brain fill with blood. Isa opened the door.

"Oh, shit," she said. "You better get that looked at."

"Christ. Say you're sorry, why don't you?"

"You first," Isa said. And we left it at that.

I found it hard to hold a pen all afternoon and I winced while erasing the chalkboard. John Hill, from the back of the class, made a show of concern. "Them football injuries are tough," he announced, "even if you're just playing Madden on Xbox like Teach."

I decided to go by the health care unit and get someone to look at my fingers. After work, Isa and Liz walked out of the building together as I fumbled with my keys. I had to try three different doors on the Health Care Unit before I found one that would open. The officer in the glass control room buzzed me into the subsequent foyer, where half a dozen inmates in various states of unshaven disrepair slouched over plastic seats. Nobody stepped up to help me, and I wandered through a nest of hallways until I found a pleasant-looking nurse my mother's age reading *Us* magazine and eating a Snickers bar. "Excuse me," I said. "My name's Brant Gilmour, from over in education. I've got a bit of a thing here with my hand and I was hoping I could find someone to look at it."

The nurse rose without introducing herself. I could see one side of her mouth finishing the candy bar as she pointed me to a chair. I saw the I.D. clamped to her collar and said, "My mother's name is Marie."

"She sounds like a wonderful woman." The nurse smiled. "Now which hand is it?"

"This one." I held it out and Marie Simmons squeezed it like a delicate beanbag, which made me rock back and forth in my chair.

"Can you make a fist?"

"Can I make a fist?" I repeated. I imitated Bruce Lee, held my fist up like a torch in front of my face. "On a good day, I can put this through a car door."

"Well, except for that ugly face you're making, you look okay to me."

"I can't do kung fu if I can't use my face."

"Well, you seem able to laugh at least. What happened? Did you try to put this through a car door? You bruise it carrying something? Drop something on it?"

"My girlfriend slammed a door on it."

"Oh, it's a finger problem. You pointed your finger where it didn't belong."

"Something like that."

"Well, don't do that. That's my medical advice."

I smiled at her. "They let anyone into medical school these days, don't they?"

She smiled back. "It's the fault of our schools," she said. "We have teachers who can't teach."

"Maybe you should hold my hand again. That was fun."

She eyed my I.D. "Mr. Gilmour, if you're going to flirt with me, you should remember where this conversation started, which was you telling me how your girlfriend smashed your hand with a door."

"Was I being unprofessional?" I said. "It's just, I got swept up in my feelings when you saved my life. You nurses must get that all the time."

"Working at this place, you wouldn't believe the B.S. I have to put up with. But it's been fun. Maybe we can talk again. Hopefully when you don't have a bruised hand. Maybe in fifteen years or so, when you're a little more mature."

"You're really good," I said. "Honestly, I'm not joking now—I've never enjoyed a trip to the doctor more."

"That's because I'm not a doctor," Marie Simmons said. "I'm an R.N."

"Let me ask you one more thing."

"Okay."

"Medically speaking," I said, "if my girlfriend may or may not have done something really questionable—but it was before I met her and she's really ashamed of it—should I ask about it? Can we be together if there's something big about her I don't know?"

"Medically speaking," Marie Simmons said, "I'm going to tell you: there's a lot you don't know about her. Because you're a guy and because you're only twenty years old. Give her time and she'll tell you. Don't try and interrogate her."

"That sounds like good advice."

"There is a technique they teach us in nursing. For how to get patient histories."

"What is it?"

"It's called listening." Marie Simmons smiled, got me to my feet, and escorted me to the door. "I'm going to finish my magazine now." She slowly shut the door on my smiling face and waved good-bye through the window.

I took a few steps down the hall, then came back and knocked on the window. Marie Simmons motioned me to open the door. "Do I have to say I'm sorry?" I asked.

"For taking up my lunch break? You can if you want, but it's okay either way."

"No," I said, "to my girlfriend."

"Let me think." Marie Simmons looked at me and then nodded. "You better. Loudly and often."

"Thanks," I said.

"Door," she said, and made a closing motion.

I took the nurse's advice, and Isa seemed surprised but pleased. In any case, she agreed to come home for Thanksgiving with me. "Will we have to travel all the way to your home planet?" she asked.

"Now how many times have I told you? I'm from Columbus. It's halfway between here and Evansville, where you're from. You'll be right at home."

"I'll believe it when I see it."

"There's still a month before Thanksgiving. I'll go home one weekend and prepare the rest of the pack."

"Because you were raised by wolves?" Isa said. "Nice. I figured nothing would be easy."

MARIE SIMMONS:
Like a Brick Shithouse

As far as prisons go, Plainfield used to be a nice one, but it's gotten so I hate to even set foot in it. It was never what you call homey, but it used to have good people. Now they've all retired or quit except me and it's run by that asshole superintendent up from Kentucky. The super got rid of all the push mowers so now they ride choppers over the property at ten miles an hour and the grass looks like sandpaper except above the sewer, where it's the color of watermelon rinds. The facility itself hasn't changed, of course, but it goes to show that "built like a brick shithouse" may be a compliment for a football player but doesn't say much for a state building.

There's not a single nurse here who's been here longer than me, though I'm only forty-eight. I'm not the youngest, and not the oldest, but I'm the best and all the doctors know it. The other day I was talking with Dr. Cramer, this young guy who looks like he sleeps in his car—a doctor, but he's still got acne and looks fifteen years old. He said, "Marie, I don't know why a woman like you works here. Don't you, honestly, get tired of men looking at your ass all day?" And I said I liked to do good, and a little attention never hurt anyone—which I thought was true, though now I hate the fact that an inmate is going to cost me my job. Or might.

There's a big turnover for doctors, though it looks like easy work—no hand-holding or complicated prescriptions. You might call it preventative medicine because the general practice is all about minimizing office visits. If an offender has a complaint, make him wait a week and then charge him five dollars if he comes in. That prevents a lot of complaints. Most of the headaches and shivers are gone by then, and you don't have to deal with all the lonely men who just want attention. When they make 67 cents a day, five dollars is a lot of money. It's enough to keep guys from sitting in the hallways complaining about a headache.

The ones that stick it out, who spend the five dollars, you see for fifteen minutes; you try to piece together some kind of medical history, then give them some ibuprofen (which half of them call I.B. Profin) and send them on their way, which is not really a "way" but back to their dorm. You don't really send someone on his way unless he's going home or you think he might be dying, in which case you call an ambulance to take him to Wishard Hospital. Nobody dies on the prison property. He might die en route to Wishard, but the book says even if he's gray and cold, any offender is supposed to get CPR until he's off the grounds at least. Actually, that's not in the book, but it's in training. Every death at the facility makes us look bad and counts against us at some level, though it probably wouldn't ever trickle down to me unless I was the person in the room.

I was the only person in the room with five inmates the day one of them decided to fuck with me and my life. Which is not to say inmates are not people, but there is definitely an us-against-them mentality. At least there was on that day. I mean, this guy didn't take me seriously as a person. He knew about my granddaughter and everything but still decided I was a joke he could laugh at. He thought I'd gone to school and worked twenty years so I could give everything I ever earned to pay for his own wasted life, but I showed him. Maybe.

Since Plainfield is just outside Indianapolis, it's become a kind of elephant's graveyard where all the old dialysis patients and a lot of the diabetics get sent. It's not too hard to ship them off to Wishard or another hospital if we have to. Not like at Michigan City which is in the middle of nowhere outside Gary. In Plainfield there's a whole fleet of wheelchair pushers carting these guys around the camp. They had to tear up a bunch of sidewalk last year because it wasn't wide enough to accommodate two wheelchairs going in opposite directions. That's the kind of camp this is: two-thirds of the offenders look like GI Joe dolls in tight T-shirts and ten-pound work boots. They hit the gym every day and strut around with their big, oiled biceps swinging. Then you got a third of the population with basically dishrags for internal organs, the kind of diabetes brought on by being fat and drinking, or the kind of bodies that skipped middle age and went from being thirty years old to sixty overnight. Maybe not exactly overnight, but it just takes a Christmas or two locked up, of sleeping in a painted concrete room with fifty other sex offenders or drug dealers or drunk drivers, just a metal bunk with no box springs. A lot of men's faces lose their joy and get a bit slack. Their hair gets gray. The insides follow. That's the way it is.

Besides the weightlifters, the rest of the guys are young bucks, so young that they think they don't have to lift weights; they feel invincible as soon as they wake up in the morning. A lot of those guys are from boys' school and are used to running the system with cries of child abuse and general adolescent loudness. They're in their twenties and don't think they're ever going to die except in the gym when basketball games turn into subtle boxing matches, elbows knocking noses and people sliding sideways across the wood floor. These guys haven't learned what work is yet. Most guys who start prison that young have never had a real job.

If you're willing to get up every morning and go to a job you hate, you've already got a lifetime of wisdom most of these guys never have. It galls me, infuriates me, to think that one of these guys can take my job away from me. Six years I went to school nights and weekends, working a cash register during the day, to be a nurse. Twenty years I've been doing it. I'm a good nurse. I'm the kind that guys ask for and not on account of my looks because I'm not that good looking. I'm a forty-eight-year-old grandmother. And now some piece of shit drug dealer who is spending his sentence in the law library decides to sue me and the state for $240,000 and my job. How am I supposed to pay him all that money if I don't have my job, let me ask? Like I would pay him a thing anyway. Some of these guys with the lawsuits, they think—I swear, I've heard them say it: "you just gotta shake the money tree and see what falls out." I wish I'd killed the guy when I had the chance. Then he'd have something to sue me for. Not that I'd ever really hurt anyone. I just think about it sometimes.

A typical day—I walk across the parking lot around five after seven. If it's good and foggy I'm hoping we have a fog day, when the sidewalks are closed because the towers can't see the fence. That means the rest of us, at least in the HCU (the health care unit) can get caught up on paperwork and generally sit around and talk. It's good for morale to have a day like this every once in a while, but they don't happen often. It's just often enough that you think about it every time you get into your car in the morning and there's a little mist on your windshield.

But if it's not too foggy and I know it, I go on in the front door and Brenda, if she's working, will pat me down and X-ray my lunch and purse. I don't like our nursing uniforms. People say they're more comfortable than the old starched white kind, but I think scrubs make us look like dental hygienists or like we're wearing pajamas for fat people. I may be a grandmother, but I'm not so far gone that I can't wear clothes with zippers.

After we get patted down I put my coat back on if I've got one and say hello to Sandy in personnel because her office is right there. She's got an "Elvis-a-day" calendar that she forgets to tear off so I do it for her. She likes the young Elvis, but I'm a seventies Elvis fan myself. When he was young he thought heartbreak was a hotel, but I know it's more than that. It's losing something you've spent your whole life acquiring. You can tell Elvis knew that at the end. The seventies Elvis is wondering why he surrounded himself by these people, why he's sweating like he is, why he's going bankrupt. I say hello to Sandy, then walk down to key control and get my set. My key ring is #32 and welded shut to keep the keys from disappearing. Then I wait for central to open the sally ports and I head over to the HCU.

The day I'm thinking of—the day this whole thing went to hell—started just like any other. The Elvis for the day was a thirty-year-old Elvis sitting on his horse, Rising Star. I drew chronics. They're the regulars, though nobody knows them all by name because the offenders transfer in and out or you switch shifts. The regulars are the ones with diabetes who come for insulin every day or the dialysis guys who get wheeled in three or four times a week. That morning two white racist guys were a few seats apart from the three other guys waiting. The littler white one looked like the Notre Dame mascot, with a pointed leprechaun beard and bushy hair that stuck out over his eyebrows. He was probably a foot shorter than his companion, who didn't have a hair on his head and looked like a bony ghost. This tall boy had rings around his eyes and a huge Adam's apple. Another white guy sat a few chairs away, but he was just holding his elbows and staring at his boots. Two black guys sat facing the reception desk, watching the officer direct traffic. One of the black guys was well over six-four and had a shiny bald head. The other had heavy braids but looked around forty, a bit shorter, a bit beaten down by life. I read off my clipboard and the tall, bony white guy followed me into the examining cabinet.

"So, how you feeling?"

"Not bad. Not bad." He sat on the table like he'd done this every day of his life. I could see the Irish flag on his bicep, which is how I knew for sure he was white brotherhood. It's a kind of code. Nobody can wear a swastika in public anymore, but Pancho Villa would be more Irish than this guy, whose last name was Zebrowski.

He held out a tattooed wrist and I took some blood for the ALT test. He had hepatitis, which meant his blood and muscles were poisoned. His blood might as well have been gasoline for all the good it did him, pumping from his head to his bony feet. He was going to die, but maybe not too soon, and he seemed cool with it all, just watching me take my sample. "That your daughter?" He lifted one hand up to point to a photo above my station: Amy in a pale blue dress and white stockings.

"My granddaughter. Doesn't she look like Alice in Wonderland?"

He leaned toward the photo. "You're not old enough to have a granddaughter."

"Don't start. I'm plenty old enough. She's eight now."

"You're kidding."

"My daughter started early. She was nineteen."

Zebrowski nodded. "I've got a two-year-old at home. A little girl."

"Well, you're twenty-five. That's about right."

"Nothing right about it. It ain't right to be locked up while your kid is growing. I'm missing everything—talked to her on the phone last night. My baby mama held the phone up to her, you know what I mean? I just want to get home."

"Yeah."

"She means everything in the world to me."

"Good." I held his wrist. "She should."

"That's why I don't let this place get to me. Shit, someone could walk up and take a crap on my lunch tray and I wouldn't say a word. I'm not about to start a fight, get sent to the hole. Ain't nothing in this camp worth losing time over."

"It's good you know that. She probably misses you."

"I'm not saying I wouldn't get even. You know how it is. But I wouldn't just start swinging."

"You do what you have to do."

"I'd do it while everyone's asleep." Zebrowski gave me a jack-o'-lantern grin, empty and bright in the same way. "Then again, maybe I'd just let it go. If it was only something a guy said, I'd let it go."

"If you can't let things go, you'll be here a long time."

"If I wanted to throw down every loudmouth asshole in this place, I couldn't even sleep on Sundays. Be too busy, know what I mean?"

When I was done sticking him, I broke off the needle in

the plastic jug we have for that kind of trash. At the end of every shift, we have sharps count. If any needles or instruments come up missing, we don't go home. We stay until it's turned up. Irish Zebrowski was chewing some non-existent gum, which made me nervous, but then he said something I didn't expect, which was that, all things considered, he was glad he had hepatitis because it meant he'd be dead soon and he wouldn't ruin his daughter's life, not the slow-motion way he was bound to destroy it otherwise. "I love her. She's the best thing that ever happened to me. The only single, unqualified good, you know? And I hate her mother. Her mother's a whore and I'm a fuck-up and I've never had a normal job. I can't see myself ever going to her grade school someday, meeting her teacher, with all these tattoos on my neck. I know what that teacher would think of my girl then. When I caught this case, I had a meth lab in the house, could have set us all on fire in half a second. She was asleep when the cops came through the door. She started screaming when the cops were yelling at me and everyone else to get on the ground. But I guess she liked the blue and red lights on the cars when I was being taken away. Her mama told me that later."

"Well, you're going to live for a while yet, so you'd better be thinking of how you can make a difference for her." I lay my clipboard on the table beside him. "You can still make a difference."

"Here's how far gone I was." Zebrowski raised one elbow. The sleeve of tattoos he had was hairless and shiny in the light. "See this one here? This Irish flag? I gave her a little one. Just like it. She's two."

"You're not even Irish. Your name's Zebrowski."

He blinked at me. Then he looked away. "My mother's Irish."

Someone knocked on the window of my door. I turned to see the little white guy standing there. He was holding up a paper towel that looked red with blood. "Just a minute," I told Zebrowski. I opened the door and the bearded man coughed again into his paper towel. I peered down his throat, then pointed to a chair. "I'm going to give you the bump test. You remember that?"

He folded his paper towel into the palm of his hand. "Not really."

"Give me a minute." I steered him, without touching him, toward the chair. "One minute." When I got back to Zebrowski, I saw that he was watching everything. He looked like a human lizard, his eyes moving but his body completely still. "We're done for now," I said. "Just have a seat out there and we'll wait for Doctor Rowe."

Zebrowski slid to his feet. "Thanks for talking with me."

"My pleasure."

As he neared the door, I slipped his file into the doctor's waiting rack, then passed my hands over my prep area. I had set out three needles wrapped in plastic. One for Zebrowski. Two for my insulin patients in the waiting room. Zebrowski's was destroyed, but when I pushed things into place, I found that one of the other packages was just empty plastic. My heart pinwheels when I make a mistake. The empty wrapper lay on the table. It looked unopened, but I could feel there was nothing inside. I usually tear the packs in two; that's how I know they're open. But maybe this one was packaged incorrectly? There were no holes in it. Then I saw that there was. A very small hole in the seam.

I went to the doorway of the examining room and saw Zebrowski sitting, watching me with his telescoping eyes, not blinking. I opened the door and the smaller Irishman rose quickly. "You're talking about TB?" he said. I leaned around him to signal the officer at the desk.

"Mister Sykes—I need a search. This area. All these men. Starting with these two."

We found the needle stuck between the seat and the frame of a waiting room chair, one nobody had been sitting in, but not far from Zebrowski. "A needle in a haystack," the officer said several times, though nobody laughed. He'd radioed for support, and another officer stood with the chronics while Officer Sykes patted them down one at a time on the far side of the room. I'm the one who found the needle. We decided to write up Zebrowski anyway, even if he would beat it when it came to the discipline board. "We don't need tattoo artists with hepatitis stealing needles," I said to myself, though I was thinking mostly about the way he'd looked at my granddaughter's picture. I picked up my clipboard and called the next offender in. It was one of the black guys there for his insulin, and he sat down wordlessly, glancing up with yellow, catlike eyes from beneath his braids.

"How are you feeling?" I asked him, and I pulled Amy's picture off my memo board and slid it into my breast pocket. In the picture, she was smiling at my former son-in-law, which was nice to see, even though of course she couldn't know what a lying whoremonger he would turn out to be.

"Fine, ma'am. That's a nice-looking little girl."

"Yes, she is. You need your insulin?"

"You going to give me all that? That looks like a lot."

"That's what it says."

"All right."

He was a quiet one, this one, unlike Zebrowski, and I had the impression he was only talking about Amy to do me a favor somehow, though I couldn't say in what way. He had a pool of silence around him; you could tell he was one of those offenders that other offenders went to for advice. He didn't have skin covered with tattoos. He rolled his T-shirt up to his shoulder, and I saw how small his wrists were. His entire body, actually, except for his troubling eyes and small potbelly, seemed childlike. "Are you new here?" he asked me.

"No," I said, "I usually work second shift."

"I'm surprised you had a picture of your family up. A lot of people, they don't want no inmates looking at their family, you know? Like we don't got none ourselves."

"I don't feel that way." The needle sank into his skin and he closed his eyes as the plunger crept forward. I always liked to put a little picture or two of home at my work station; it kept me from being institutionalized, and I think it made guys treat me like a person instead of like a pill dispenser with an ass. No one would ever walk out of this place and recognize my granddaughter from this old picture. My daughter had insisted I get an unlisted phone number a few years back though.

"Are you okay?" I patted the man on the shoulder after I removed the needle. For some of these men, a nurse is the only person to touch them in years. Most of them are like puppy dogs inside and melt at a fingertip on their arm.

"That just seemed like a lot," the man said, "but I guess the doctor has his reasons."

"I should hope so."

"All right." He rose and touched his tricep. "See you tomorrow."

"See you tomorrow. Thank you for being such a gentleman, Mr. Taylor."

"Taylor?" The man stopped halfway to the door. "I'm Thomas. Joe Thomas. That's Taylor out there. The bald guy."

"What?"

"Oh shit." The man put the palm of his hand over his tricep. "What have you done to me?"

Two days later my supervisor called me at home to say, "You're getting sued. But don't worry. I've been sued probably twenty times. Nothing will come of it." And I know that nothing will probably happen. Nobody died. It'll be hard for anyone to prove I gave the guy too much insulin. All I need to do is lie, but I hate to do that. I don't want to be that person, one more person these guys can look at and say, "She's just like us, but she didn't get caught." I want them to know not everyone is like that. But it would take me eight years to bring home $240,000 and how am I going to do that with no job? I made a mistake, but so did this guy— Thomas. He's getting free health care, for Christ's sake. He's already getting something for nothing. My daughter has to pay a fifth of her paycheck to insure her and Amy. So I made a mistake. Why should I lose everything? I said this to my supervisor, with his door closed. He just shook his head at me, then pulled his stethoscope free and tossed it into a drawer. "Look where you are," he said. "You're in a prison. This place is all about making a mistake and losing everything. Listen: you just deny. Deny, deny, deny. All right? He's still alive. No harm, no foul. We're not here to help them win the Olympics. We're here to make sure they don't die on state property." He shook his head, then added, "We never had this conversation." He had his back to me as I rose and went back to work. I've taken his advice and so far it's held up, but I'm not happy anymore. Plainfield used to be a decent place to work, but it's gotten so you can't trust anybody.

A COOKING LESSON

Isa said:

So, during the last lockdown, they closed the school and I worked the lunch line. It went on for three days, after those guys in South Dorm refused to vacate the basketball court. The superintendent practically shut the place down. There was no movement on the walks and we weren't doing normal meals. We ran out of bologna and mustard and were just doing peanut butter and jelly sandwiches. Only then we were out of jelly. And bread too. We had hot dog buns. So we were told to make them on that. "How do you make a peanut butter and jelly sandwich with no jelly?" I remember asking, but I guess that was silly because the head cook just laughed.

"You leave out the fucking jelly," he said.

I was alone in the kitchen with Johnny Winston, the officer who used to run chow. We opened an old jar of peanut butter (and by jar, you know I mean one of those ten-pound buckets). It's so old and cracked, Winston says we can't use it at first, but it's all we can find. "Put some honey in there to soften it," he says, only we can't find any honey. Winston goes to look for some but then he doesn't come back—but

Big Larry does and he says there is no honey, so we're just going to add some cooking oil. He's got a big canister of some kind. I don't know what it is, but he pours some in the peanut butter and we stir it up. We can actually stir, once there's oil in it. It gets soft for about five minutes. But then it starts to set, and in the end we can't spread it without ripping the hot dog buns up, so we just have to tear off a piece of peanut butter and roll it between two hands, make kind of like a rope out of it and put it on a hot dog bun.

I look at Winston, who's come back, and I say, "We can't serve this. It looks like a piece of shit. I mean, this literally looks like a piece of shit. This is going to set the inmates off. They're going to burn this place down."

And Winston says, "You're right, but what else are we going to do? We don't serve them anything to eat, they'll go off for sure." And so we just stack up these trays, with all these shit-looking peanut butter sandwiches and start throwing them into paper bags, and you know what? The guys loved them. They loved those peanut butter sandwiches. I had guys telling me they never got served food as good as when they were acting up and got locked down that one time. "The Man, he was afraid," I heard one guy say. "He did us right, that time."

BRANT GILMOUR AND ISA BOONE:
Part 4

My mother was not happy to learn I was dating someone I'd met at the prison. "What kind of name is Isa?" she asked.

"Short for Isabelle. Her big sister's name is Anabelle. But I've been told repeatedly that I'm not supposed to hold that against her."

My dad held his fork over his heart and finished chewing. "What your mother's really asking is: is she black?"

"No. Would it matter?"

"Brant," my mother said.

"I'm offended you would even ask that," my dad said.

"But it was the first thing you asked me."

"Like there are a million Isas out there," my father said. "Like that's a common name. Just forget it. Forget it. We don't want to know anything more about her."

My mother crossed her legs. Her hands were folded loosely around her napkin. "Honey."

"She's white," I said. "She's from Evansville. Her folks—"

"Forget it. I don't want to know."

It took about ten minutes for me to tell them a little bit about her. That she had a bachelor's degree and lived in

Plainfield. I didn't mention that she was almost ten years older than me. My mother asked what she liked to do, what her interests were. The truth was, Isa didn't do any sports or belong to any clubs. She watched some TV and read some James Patterson and I knew she talked on her cell phone with people, but she'd never introduced me to anyone, and her apartment was all her: no empty chairs or signs that other people came to visit much at all. I showed my parents a picture, which my father inspected carefully and then smiled.

"It was taken at a friend's wedding," I explained. I'd smiled at it one night when she was showing me her photo album.

"Me in a dress." She'd laughed.

"You look great," I'd said.

"My ass makes the dress look big," she said.

"Not true," I said. "That skinny bride makes your dress look big."

"Ha. Well, she's not so skinny now. She's had two kids."

Then I insisted she take a picture of us, which she did by holding her phone at arm's length. Looking at the tiny screen, I said, "Oh, that's no good. I could be some stranger you just met in a bar." I took off my shirt and made a ridiculous smile, my nose almost touching her phone, so in the picture, my head looks five times as big as hers.

She studied the screen and smiled. "You could still be someone I just met in a bar." But in the morning, when I got dressed to leave, I found that wedding party picture on top of my jeans with a turquoise post-it note that read, *You make me want to wear a dress. Thanx. Isa.*

I took her cell phone and left her a picture of her asleep and then one of me giving her a thumbs-up.

"That's her beside the bride," I told my parents.

"Those dresses are always so hideous," my mother said. "What is that color?"

I looked again. "Sea taffy, I think she said."

"Lord. But she looks pretty, Brant."

"I thought she would be some short-haired, mustached brute," my father said. "Wear overalls."

"She's got some nice coveralls, but she only wears them when she's welding," I said. "Hey, that reminds me. Come take a look at my truck, Dad. Isa did some body work on it."

"What?" My dad's back stiffened; his jaw pointed to the window and driveway.

"She's not a lesbian, Dad." And I smiled at my plate. "She's so not a lesbian."

"What's it like, Brant? Working in a prison?" My mother had carried in two cups of coffee, but because I was now a grown man out of school and living on my own, she was letting me drink my Diet Coke without comment, though she looked unhappy at the sight of the can beside her nice plates. "Do inmates ever apologize to you?"

"To me? What for?"

"For their crimes. Do they show remorse?"

"Why would they show remorse to me? I'm their writing teacher."

"Don't you make them write about their lives?"

I looked from my mother to my father. "It's really none of my business," I said.

"He teaches them how to pass the GED," my father said. "Isn't that right? There's no remorse on the GED."

"That's right," I said, and I thought about what I could tell my mother. I couldn't ask my students about their crimes. If they told me things, I couldn't believe them. And there are only so many times in life a man can apologize for the same thing. I'd read Simon Wiesenthal's *The Sunflower* in college and I was a big believer that an apology had to be handmade and it wasn't up to me to forgive someone for all the hurts weathered by the Jews of World War II or for anything that hadn't been done to me personally. I didn't know what my mother expected, that men who were guilty of selling drugs were going to apologize to me, a white unmarried college boy, years later.

"I can think of three apologies I've heard at work," I said.

"Three?"

Englehart had worked a year at a privatized prison; it was in a converted cereal factory in Indianapolis. The walls were windowless cinderblock and the exercise yard was a chain-link box in a corner of the parking lot. The corporation was too cheap to buy the inmates coats, and so from November to March, outdoor recreation was a concrete dayroom on the fifth floor because it had a skylight the officer would open for air.

Englehart used to work the disciplinary unit, and one time he got an inmate who was being segregated for bit-ing an officer, a sergeant Englehart liked. The segregation offenders were kept in tiny rooms with slotted, windowed doors they couldn't see out of. Once a day, they were allowed to walk around a common room, but Englehart said he worked around this by waking his man up at three-thirty in the morning and asking if the guy wanted to go for a walk. When the guy screamed at him, Englehart would log in: "Declined recreation."

He'd also read the guy's mail and then make comments about a sister or a girlfriend he'd read about, acting as if he'd met this girl at a bar. This wasn't technically illegal because officers in segregation were allowed to "skim" everything except legal mail—ostensibly, to make sure it didn't involve plans to escape.

"But the best," Englehart had told me, "is when I fuck with their food. They hate that." I asked him what he meant, and he said, "Actually, I only did this with that guy who bit a sergeant I liked. He bit him! Like a fucking lion. I saw the scar. But I'd serve the food tray through the slot. The tray's got a plastic lid on it. And he'd lift that lid to see that the tray was empty. He'd start yelling 'Someone ate my applesauce! Where's my fucking dinner?' and I'd just smile in that little window and say, 'I'm sorry, man. I'm sure it was full when I put it in there. You must have eaten it real fast and now you're messing with me. Sorry. I'm real sorry, but I can't help you.'" Englehart added: "I don't care how big and bad a motherfucker is. Take away his thirty cents worth of applesauce and bologna when he doesn't expect it and he starts being sorry he came to prison."

"You like that?" I'd asked him.

"I feel a little bad," Englehart said, "telling you about it now. But at the time it seemed like justice."

That was the first apology I'd ever heard in prison. "Not much of one," my mother said. "That's horrible."

"It's an imperfect world," I said.

"What're the other two?" my dad asked.

I had a student in literacy class, Washington Graham—a slender black man, maybe 180 pounds, who had incredible biceps. Each of his arms was as big around as two beer cans. He also had a huge smile and a self-effacing giggle like a little boy. His first day of class, he told me he couldn't read that well but he'd been praying about it. He really wanted to learn, he said, and he prayed that this time he wouldn't quit or get discouraged—that this time it would be different.

I said to him something I'd started saying: "You just come to class every day and we'll read together, all right? If you read for forty minutes a day, how can you not be a better reader at the end of two months?" And that seemed reasonable enough to both of us. And even though I had twelve other students, I managed to spend thirty to forty minutes a day with Graham. He often checked thick books out of the library because he liked to be seen carrying them back and forth, but in class he and I would sit with articles and stories written at a second or third grade level. He read them in front of me and if the story came with comprehension questions, he would read all the multiple choices, saying after each one, "No, that ain't right. That don't sound right." But all the time, he watched my face carefully for clues. He knew his phonics, but he really had trouble remembering the beginning of a sentence he'd just read.

One day, he got a long letter from the courts, and he half-hid the envelope for a while, then asked me to read it and tell him what it said. The courts were rejecting a request for sentence modification and I told him so, but only after I'd figured that out, which meant I read about an afternoon when he and two friends had broken into a man's house and beaten the man with a shotgun while the man's girlfriend screamed from the couch. Washington Graham had been arrested in the back seat of the getaway car. His companions had fled on foot when police cars blocked the alley. It didn't seem like the person I sat with every day, the one who was so proud of learning his multiplication tables and who always took a seat alone in the corner and smiled at almost everything. When I told him the judge had denied his modification, he looked me in the eyes to see how much I knew about him. When I didn't look away, he looked down and said, "I thought they were my friends."

Every six weeks or so, I would send him to take the achievement test. We raised his math scores some, but his reading hovered at third or fourth grade. I was under pressure to kick him out because he had been in school for half a year and shown so little progress. When the waiting list got too long, the director came to me with my roster and pointed to Washington Graham's name. "Can he pass this test or not? Yes or no?"

And I had to say I really didn't know, but maybe not.

The next week Graham was removed from class. He wouldn't shake my hand as he was leaving. One time, weeks before, when all the students had left, I found this note on his desk next to a dictionary:

I am so fucken dum it don't make cents petty. It's crazy I wish I will never stop school because it hard for me in heir. It make me fascination I'm so tried of it. My mind is gone so far in the ground were it need to stay.

I am a sorry man cann't Learn anything. I'm tried 28 year old and dum as hell

Graham
9-4-09
Looser
Loser
Loser
I know that
for myself.
fuck up.

"That's terrible," my mother said.

"What's the last apology you heard?" my dad said.

"Graham was walking away," I said. "I told him I was sorry."

We had a lovely Thanksgiving. My sister had stayed at college, which was nice because she was insufferable with pride at pledging the Tri-Delts. My Aunt Susie and Uncle Grady came. Isa made a great impression on everyone, despite the fact that she couldn't cook and so we didn't bring anything and she was terrible at doing dishes, as if she'd never held a sink brush before. Isa has a big personality and most of the women in my family don't, so it was fun. People seemed to like her, though I found out later that things were said out of earshot. My mother thought Isa was holding me back. But I didn't know that when we walked out into the driveway and waved good-bye, both of us stuffed with the usual potatoes and poultry.

We drove back to my apartment downtown. My building was peaceful in the afternoon. Most of the tenants were visiting their families, and the old people who remained were quietly creaking on the floorboards, televisions chirping through the doors. Isa and I unbuttoned our jeans and lay back on my bed, our feet hanging to the floor and the afternoon light softly making window panes on the bed. I put on some James Taylor. Isa kicked off her jeans and said, "God, I'm fat," but then squeezed my bicep and dug her chin into my shoulder happily and prepared to fall asleep.

Before I closed my eyes, I found myself saying, "Did you have fun?"

"Yeah. You?"

"Yeah."

"You have a nice family," she said.

"You know what bothered me?" I said.

"What?"

My Aunt Susie had told a story about leaving her purse at Kroger's. She'd had to stop at my parents' house and use the phone to call (because her cell phone was in her purse), but then it turned out that she hadn't left the purse at the register, but in her cart. And she'd left her cart in the parking lot. But when she called, the store manager said he had the purse in his office and she went and picked it up and everything inside was just as she'd left it. "So you see," she'd said. "There are still good people."

"What bothered you about that?" Isa asked.

"My first thought, when Susie told that story, was: why is my aunt lying to us? What does she hope to gain from telling us this bullshit story about her purse?"

"You thought that?"

"Yeah. Isn't that messed up?"

Isa sat up. "You're institutionalized. That's prison thinking. That's criminal thinking."

"Really? You didn't think anything like that?"

"No."

"I feel kind of bad."

Isa laughed. "No, Brant. I thought: she must not have had anything good in there."

"What's wrong with us? Why are we so suspicious?"

"I blame society," Isa said. "It's not us. It's the world."

We fell asleep. But I had the suspicion that it wasn't the

world. It was Isa. And now me. My father, whenever I'd come to him as a kid and said that something around the house was broken, would always respond the same way. "Operator error," he'd say. He wasn't always right, but I lay in bed that Thanksgiving and thought about the world and my new response to it, my disbelief in kindness, and it seemed that most of the people I knew were happier than me and Isa. My dad's words echoed in my head.

BRANT GILMOUR AND ISA BOONE:
Part 5

I had noticed the head trainer at the YMCA where I worked out because she greeted everyone who came in the door, but she didn't interest me in more than a friendly way. I'd seen her behind the counter signing people up, and she seemed like one of those people who thought she should be in Hollywood or somewhere else—wherever the person she was talking to on the phone was. She had a huge keychain with a rubber soccer ball and a ton of keys. She wore sunglasses all the time, even in the gym, which I thought was ridiculous until one evening she pulled them off to squint in the mirror and I saw that she had a glass eye. After that I found myself thinking she was nice, which, of course, made no sense at all.

And then one morning—one Saturday, early—we were basically the only two people in the weight room. She was working out herself and I noticed the bright, hard shape of her spandex as she climbed onto the leg machine. Her awkward machine was opposite the one where I was doing my military press. She pushed her knees together and then let them float apart, her ankles in the air. Her legs separated, quivering, like a warm valentine being torn in two. She pushed them back together, breathing out, her bare shoulders shaking. Her sunglasses looked up and I saw my eyes reflected in them and she smiled. Half an hour later, we were standing by the water fountain together. "Why anyone would buy a sports drink is beyond me," she said. "Water is so delicious."

"It is good to drink," I said. "But I really wish we had a pool here."

"The Y on 86th has one. It's all right."

"But it's on 86th."

"True." She seemed unsure where to go with that idea, beyond agreeing with me. "I'm K.P."

"Brant." We shook hands. Her hand was warm. "Actually, I'm done. I'm on my way home."

"Me, too. I'm not working today. Just working out." She pointed toward the coat nook, where a sweatshirt and gym bag formed a turquoise and white pile on the floor.

We were already by the door to the lockers, so I stopped uncertainly and said, "See you around?"

"I hope so," she said.

"Why don't you work out?" I asked Isa. "I don't mean because you need to. I'm not saying that. I mean, just because it's fun."

"Because it's not fun. It's the opposite of fun. Actually, putting on tight clothes and sweating in public is what I would consider anti-fun."

"Well, you could wear what you wanted. But I mean, why don't you have any hobbies? Why don't you ever want to go do anything?"

Isa turned her eyes from me. "I don't have any hobbies? What are you getting at, Brant?"

"I don't know. Do you? What are things you like to do? All we ever do is have sex, eat fast food, watch movies and TV."

"That's called life," Isa said. "It's what people do, who work for a living. We don't spend our weekends jumping out of planes."

"I know that, but . . ."

"I'm sorry I'm boring you," Isa said. "Why don't you find someone who likes hang gliding or bungee jumping. Or lifting weights up and down, if you find that so exciting."

A few days later we were alone in my classroom, watching inmates walk laps in the exercise yard outside the window.

"Sometimes I don't want you to work out," Isa said, "because when you do, I know someday you'll leave me."

"I won't leave you. That's crazy. We're good. We're happy. Aren't we? Aren't you happy?"

"Let's talk about something else."

"Talking about happiness is so depressing," I said.

"I am happy," Isa said. "But when I see you working out, I know you're not going to stay here. You're getting ready for something that doesn't exist here."

"What doesn't exist here?" I said. Isa and I had talked a

few times about how the prison was like a medieval village. It was completely self-contained, with its own barber shop, post office, doctor's office, police, a store, and no competition. It was a village with its own mayor and sheriff and local politics—but no women or children.

"The future," Isa said.

Isa and I never touched or even walked within a couple feet of each other at the prison. We tried not to look like we were sleeping together. Isa said she didn't give a shit what inmates said about her, but she liked it better when they weren't right.

We had seen an old man and a balding woman leaning together on the wrought iron fence outside a church one weekend. They were holding hands and watching someone, a grandchild, I guessed, on the playground. "Isn't that sweet?" Isa had said.

"Really?" I said. "You like holding hands?"

"I don't like doing it," Isa said, "but that doesn't mean I don't like it. I don't like jazz music, but I like pictures of Chet Baker."

That afternoon at McDonald's, I reached across the tiny table and squeezed Isa's hand as she held a fry into some ketchup. She looked up like I'd slapped her and she pulled away.

"What's wrong?"

"Nothing," she said. "Just don't do that."

"What?"

"Try to hold my hand and stuff. We're not in third grade."

Isa ate her fries and held her hands away from me.

"Isa," I said. "You think hand-holding is for little kids and old people. But no one in-between?"

"I just don't like it, Brant. Don't you understand?"

"Not really."

"Sometimes I think: if you hold my hand here, then after we break up those kids working the register are going to feel sorry for me when I'm sitting here by myself. That's why."

"Isa, is that how you walk around? Thinking like that?"

"Brant, I'm thirty-two. I work in a prison. I know what men are like."

"Well, thanks a lot. For establishing that I'm just like an inmate."

"That's what you always say though, isn't it, Brant? That we're all the same? One big happy family? A family of humanity? Well, you can't have the one without the other. I'm just pessimistic. But I'm hoping you prove me wrong. Can you promise me that? Will you promise not to let me down?"

I looked her in the eyes, but before I could speak, she tapped the back of my hand, flattened my hand against the table.

"Please, Brant. For both of us. Don't say anything."

OVERHEARD:
Two Students

1: You know something?
2: What?
1: I got eight brothers and sisters.
   My folks are still married.
   I'm thirty-six years old
   and I'll be the first one of all of us to get his GED.
2: Shit, man.
1: Yeah.
2: You got eight brothers and sisters?
1: Yeah.
2: And your two parents still alive?
1: That's right.
2: And you the smartest out of all of them?
   That's the saddest thing I ever heard.
1: Fuck you, man.
2: That's all right, man.
   I'm still proud of you.

BRANT GILMOUR AND ISA BOONE:
Part 6

Isa's big sister surprised me by being older than her, which shouldn't have surprised me at all, but Isa was thirty-two to my twenty-two and her sister was middle-aged. Anabelle had the heavy-shouldered, overly made-up look of a woman who was unsuccessfully showing a house. She was holding one cigarette over the ashy corpses of two others when I came in. She looked me over toe to head and smiled, but she didn't get up from the couch, as if she were afraid that putting her coffee down would allow some precious fire to go out.

"Cute," she said to Isa. She held out a hand to me. "I've heard a lot about you." Her hand was cold.

"Isa says you're not to be believed. About anything. Which makes me think I'd like to buy you a drink and ask about this one's high school days."

Anabelle snorted. "High school? That was a hundred years ago for some of us."

"Well," I said. "Pretend I'm doing an oral history on the age of radio. No, tell me about high school and where you were when Kennedy was shot."

Anabelle smiled sideways and crushed her cigarette. "I like him, Isa. He's smart."

"Smart ass," Isa said, "but that's close enough for me."

"So, why're you with my sister?" Anabelle asked me. "You like older girls?"

"I like Isa," I said. "That so hard to believe?"

"How long you known her?"

"Since March. Eight months."

"Yeah," Anabelle said. "It is."

When we entered the mall parking lot, Isa warned me that her niece was fourteen going on nineteen. "She dresses like she's on her way home from a fraternity party."

Anabelle shook her head. "It's not that bad."

"Okay. She dresses like—never mind."

"You should try having kids," Anabelle said. "By the way, are you thinking of it? Isa's not getting any younger."

Isa glared through the windshield. I didn't say anything.

"I guess she's got you," Anabelle said. I glanced over at Isa, who looked momentarily like she were passing a kidney stone. Her elbow lay flat and lifeless against the far window.

She finally glanced up and I mouthed the letters, "WTF?"

"I know," Isa said. "I know."

"What do you know?" Anabelle asked.

"More than you can imagine. Here." Isa leaned over my lap and honked. "There's Jinny."

I wheeled the car against the curb. A teenager with a strawberry constellation of acne at her jawline turned toward us, hunched beneath a heavy backpack. She did look mildly undressed, as if she were uncommitted to any single piece of clothing from her tangled shoelaces to her semi-unbuttoned blouse. She hurried across the sidewalk to open the car door and join her mother in the backseat. "Jinny, this is Brant. Isa's boyfriend."

"Nice to meet you," I said.

"You too," the girl said. Those were the last words she said to me, though the four of us went to Chick-fil-A and spent half an hour together. Mostly Isa and I made fun of the sinister friendliness of the Christian youth behind the counter. The teenager at our table pushed waffle fries into her low-hanging mouth with one hand and consulted her cell phone with the other. Anabelle didn't eat much of her meal. She seemed distracted, like maybe she missed the cigarette she'd left behind in the otherwise empty coin tray of my truck.

"I'm not sure about your sister," I told Isa later.

"What do you mean?"

"I'm not sure what she's after. If she's nice or not."

"Oh, for Christ's sake. She's not nice. She's my sister. Where do you think I came from?"

"You didn't climb out of the foam or jump out of the forehead of Zeus?"

"I swear I have no idea what you are talking about half the time. Look, we can't all be spoiled clueless like yourself.

Some of us come from these things called families. And these families follow us around and try to destroy us our whole lives."

"I have a family."

"So you know what I mean."

"Not really. My family loves me."

Isa stared at me. "Brant, I swear. Sometimes you make me so mad, I could just strangle you."

Isa said to me later, while we were watching TV, "You know those Penthouse Forum stories where a guy winds up sleeping with his girlfriend and her sister?"

"Let's just say I have heard of these stories," I said.

"Well, if I ever hear of you sleeping with my sister, we're through. Not because I'd be jealous. And not because you'd be an asshole. I've been with plenty of assholes. But you'd be a stupid fucking asshole with no taste, and I don't think I could live with that."

I reflected a moment, then opened one hand on my lap and offered, "You do seem like the prize in your family."

"Don't talk about my family," Isa said. "Only I can do that."

The television laughed at itself. I listened.

Then Isa cleared her throat. "But thanks. I know. Please don't hold it against me."

OVERHEARD:
Outside the Health Care Unit

1: I'm gonna write a pome, man.

2: Go 'head.

1: It's about the way we can't sit
   and eat our fucking bologna sandwiches
   under a TREE.
   Just sit under a tree.
   Like in pomes, man.

2: You miss trees?

1: Yeah, I miss them.

2: True. Not a tree in this whole camp.
   From fence to fence.
   Just that bare-ass grass
   that turns yellow in July.

1: And stays that piss color 'til April!

2: I ain't walked under no tree . . .

1: I ain't sat under no tree . . .

2: Ain't felt the shade of no tree . . .

1: Ain't lost no kites
   like motherfucking Buster Brown

in no tree . . .

2: Charlie Brown.

1: Whatever.

Ain't no trees here.

2: That's a pome.

1: I want to climb a tree.

Goddamn, I want to be a motherfucking squirrel

and climb a motherfucking tree

up over your head.

Get HIGH

but you know what I mean

I mean up in the air

though the other wouldn't bother me none, either.

2: You might hide in a tree, they gave you one.

You'd jump out—

RAHR—

like a panther!

1: I'd climb up outta this monkey ranch.

Jump the fence.

Free.

2: Well, that's why they aren't any trees, you dumb ass

motherfucker.

'Cause a people like you.

1: I'm writing this pome.

2: Aw, man. You from 38th Street.

Why don't you wish for a bus stop?

Something you know about.

1: Man, who ever heard of a pome
    'bout a bus stop?
2: Who ever heard of a drug dealer
    writing a pome
    that mattered?

A POME

The Tree

I live in a brick shithouse
sitting on a pancake
of dead lawn.

Birds pass
sometimes
sometimes
hesitate
in the chain-link fence.

But my heart is a tree
A tree
A tree
full of shade.

It grows
and grows.

BRANT GILMOUR AND ISA BOONE:
Part 7

After Englehart got fired, I'd called him once, but we
hadn't had much to say. Then, months later, he got me on
the phone. He'd decided to get a lawyer and fight it. "Karl
Whipker, L.L.C.," he read to me over the phone.

"How'd you get his name?"

"I was in the Health Care Unit one time and this nurse
said she was getting sued by an inmate. This is the name
she said. I figured he ain't afraid of the Department of
Correction."

He and I had only discussed his firing obliquely because,
quite frankly, it was embarrassing. But now he was asking if
I'd be a character witness or make some kind of statement
about his job performance. "I'm not your supervisor," I said.

"But you can write," Englehart said. "Can't you? What
am I going to do? Go in there with my state form and these
blackened-in ovals saying I'm 'average'?"

"But, I mean—you did it, didn't you?"

"Hell, yes, I did it, brother. But that's beside the point!
That's not what I'm talking about. I shouldn't have been

fired over it. It's not illegal to own tobacco in the state of Indiana."

"It's trafficking to give it to an inmate since it's a banned substance for them."

"No, it's contraband. Drugs or a cell phone would be trafficking."

"It's trafficking."

"It's contraband. Shit, they aren't supposed to have paper clips or rubber bands either. Apples are contraband, for Christ's sake. It's just a rule infraction; it's not a felony."

I didn't know what to say. He'd put the tobacco in a zip-lock bag at the bottom of a giant McDonald's cup, smuggled it through checkpoint I don't know how many times. No one at the facility could bring drinks in anymore. People hated Englehart. I heard his name every morning as people tossed their coffee into the trash.

"Were you charged with a felony?"

"No, but I was fired. They should have just given me a reprimand or something. I never had any other issues."

"What's your lawyer supposed to do?"

"He's going to get me my job back, so I can quit. Then I'm going to get a job with the State Police like I should have in the first place. Only I can't do that with this on my record. It makes me look like a criminal."

"Brother," I said, "you look a little bit like a criminal to me."

"Fuck you, Brant. You see? You see what's happening to

you? You used to be nice. When you started there, you were nice. But I told you, didn't I? You stick around there too long, you turn into an asshole. You going to do me like that? You won't even write the letter?"

"What am I going to say in it?"

Englehart didn't say anything. Then he seemed to hold the phone close to his mouth and he growled: "Why don't you say, 'Me? Oh, my goodness! I've never made a mistake in my life and I'm so special my ass smells like peaches and I know this because my fat girlfriend, who shoulda been fired herself, told me so."

"Good-bye, man."

"See you the fuck later," Englehart said. "Brother."

Two weeks later I got an envelope in the mail from a lawyer: Karl Whipker, L.L.C. I showed it to Isa that evening.

"Isa, why is Englehart doing this? All this paper could have gone into printing a fucking Gideon Bible or the *New York Times* or someone's will or something. Why does he want to lawyer up like this? Doesn't he know he's guilty?"

Isa looked at me. "Maybe you don't get the concept. That's exactly the time to lawyer it up."

"He screwed up! Can't he just accept it?"

"We've all screwed up. You're the one who's always talking all human about the offenders. Giving second chances and shit. Why not give Englehart a second chance?"

"It just bugs me."

"Why? A good question is *why*."

I thought about that for a moment. "We talked—about a month after he lost his job—and he wasn't sounding like this. He seemed sorry about what he'd done."

"One's got nothing to do with the other. This is about fairness. Getting treated fairly by the system."

"I think it's about feeling entitled. To a job or anything else." I tossed the envelope onto her lap. "Hey, did you get one?"

"A letter? Yeah. And yeah, I'll probably write something for him. He's a nice kid."

"You've got to be kidding."

"Why not? What's it cost me? Nothing. I thought he was your friend, Brant."

"I did too! That's the whole point! Why'd he have to go and do something so stupid? And why does he have to drag me into it now?"

"So don't write it," Isa said, throwing her hands up. "Be a bastard. You could use the practice. I've told you a million times that you're too nice."

At lunch the next day I called the number for Englehart's attorney and got a paralegal who said her name was Melinda Coole. "I received a letter from Mr. Whipker," I said, "on behalf of a Marvin Englehart."

"Okay."

"Well, I'm not going to write anything. I just don't want you to waste time waiting for it if you need to contact someone else."

"You sound kind of conflicted," Melinda Coole offered. "Maybe you need to take the weekend and think about it?"

"No, no. There's really nothing to think about. Are you familiar with the case? It happened months ago."

"Well, I'm sure if Mr. Whipker wrote to you, it was because Mr. Englehart thought you might be of some help."

"Maybe I could have. Before he tried to bring in a super-sized baggie of controlled substance."

"I'm really not familiar with the case."

"Should I speak with Mr. Whipker?"

"Mr. Whipker is in court."

"When will he be back in the office?"

Melinda Coole laughed. It was loud and sudden and seemed completely genuine, like it had escaped her. She coughed herself back into her speaking voice. "I'm sorry, I'm sorry. I've known Mr. Whipker for three years. Mr. Whipker is having the longest day of his life today. How 'bout I take a message and have him call you?"

"Court not going well?"

"You could say that." She laughed again. "You most certainly could. It's kind of like that joke: 'Other than that, Mrs. Lincoln, what did you think of the theatre?'"

KARL WHIPKER, L.L.C.

My mother wept when I found Jesus, but my father just said, "I didn't know he was lost." My father had little ongoing interest in my salvation and in any case considered my recent claim unconvincing because it occurred only after I'd dropped a plastic bag of cocaine in the middle of the courtroom. The handkerchief I'd been reaching for hung limply at my side, and the prosecutor and the Honorable Judge Marsha Wallace and even my client all stared at the bag on the floor until I picked it up and moved it from hand to hand. Judge Wallace asked me to approach the bench.

Everyone has heard the joke, "What do you call a hundred lawyers at the bottom of the sea?" (answer: a good start), but few people realize, as they're laughing, that this joke used to be told about black people—or, if you're from Indiana, about Kentuckians. It's the kind of joke people tell about a group they don't consider human. Let me just say: I am very human and yet there have been times when I wished I were at the bottom of the sea myself and that afternoon I spent in Marion County lock-up was certainly one of them.

My part-time paralegal, Melinda Coole, has been with

me four years and gotten me out of countless jams. She's made ten copies of my office key ring and keeps them around for all the times when I can't find mine. The afternoon in question, she bailed me out of jail within six hours, but in that time I managed to suffer a rubber-gloved cavity search and had completely fallen to pieces at least twice against the cinderblock walls. ("Oh come on," said a man who looked like he'd been rolling around in an ashtray. "It's not that bad. Just wait 'til tomorrow morning when all the alcohol is finally out of your system. That's when I start kicking the bars, personally.") Melinda Coole is my paralegal's honest and true name. My clients—who spend more time on the phone with her than they probably should, due to my erratic schedule—call her anything from MC to Coolie to Coo-Coo. Need I even state, explicitly, that because I do mostly drug crime and because the system is what it is, most of my clients are black, as well as frighteningly guilty, to be honest, though naturally all still entitled to a good defense so that the system doesn't swallow them in a flurry of legal Liquid Plumber. Melinda showed up and let me put one arm over her shoulder as she helped me to my car.

"Whip, Whip," she said. "It comes to this."

I shrugged, hoping to get a little sympathy, but she just repeated my name a few more times, shaking her head.

"Jesus, Whip, you stink!" She lifted my elbow off her shoulder. "Oh, come on. It's not that bad. Did you at least hand out a few business cards while you were in there?"

"How can you joke?" I said. As soon as we were in her

half-plastic Honda SUV, I laid my head down on her lap. "Just take me home."

"Come on, you big baby. I don't think Roger would like that." Roger was her husband, an insanely egotistical dentist, of all things—as if someone who spends his life putting his fingers in other people's mouths has anything to feel superior about.

"I don't mean your home," I said. "I just mean some place that feels like home, some place warm and kind."

"There's no such place," Melinda said. "No such place, baby." She laughed and left the keys dangling from the ignition. Her fingers were warm on my growing bald spot. She refrained from her usual laugh, which was a hands-on-the-hips pirate laugh that our clients liked. For me, today, she used her quiet laugh: a laugh like none of the misbehavior around her really bothered her because she had somewhere to go afterward no matter how late it was.

I made as though I were wiping my tears dry on her jeans.

"Don't get too friendly," she said. "You only pay me eighteen bucks an hour."

Then I sat up and said, "So where are we going?"

"I'm going home," she said, "but I thought I'd drop you off at the office. Figured you'd want to wash up. And you do have a four-thirty appointment—the Parker divorce. Your usual sales pitch. I'd have cancelled it for you, but obviously I've been a bit busy, what with the bail bondsman and all. Oh, and that reminds me: the reason we're in my car is that yours got towed when the meter ran out. It's at the impound lot on Delaware Street. Can you remember that?"

I groaned. "How do I look?"

Melinda glanced me over. "I wouldn't want you handling my divorce," she said, "but I guess that goes without saying."

She dropped me off at my office, which was a taffy-colored cinderblock building. ("The latest in bunker technology—think 'shock-and-awe, shock-and-awe'," Melinda had said in her sarcastic tours of the office for a temp or two I'd had over the years.) There were a couple of bullet holes above the front window, but that was a side effect of our prime location a few blocks from the city/county building and the police station. I got the door open. Melinda pulled away with a sassy blat-blat on the horn that made me tremble, but then she swung back to the curb and clacked her fingernails against the window. It hummed down.

"Hey, Whip," she said. "I almost forgot. Your four-thirty? She left a message on your cell phone. She wants to take you to dinner."

"I see," I said, taking the phone from Melinda and leaning toward her open window. Melinda gave me a sad look, then licked her fingertips and started to press down my hair, then laughed and palmed my forehead.

"You better not fuck her," she said and laughed her big, open-mouthed laugh. Her SUV slid away from the curb with her elbow out the window.

This was not the moment I found Jesus, though I was beginning to resemble him physically. I had acquired a somewhat tortured look like a medieval icon, and it had been thirty hours since I'd shaved. I usually made a point of shaving before court, but this morning had been particularly rough, the high point being a ropelike but not inedible bagel I'd found beneath the seat of my now vanished car. I was a firm believer that with enough butter or Tabasco, a bachelor could eat anything. Now, however, my stomach was starting to work against me; I had been too slow to get any of the paper-bagged bologna sandwiches the officers had thrown into the lock-up. The tiny sandwiches had disappeared into the giant hands of inner city youth who all seemed to know each other.

I found myself hoping that Tess Parker, my four-thirty appointment, was serious about taking me to dinner. I was also hoping that, despite whatever promises I might have made before, we could come to a lucrative enough arrangement to help me get myself a lawyer—since, according to the Honorable Judge Marsha Wallace, I would be needing one.

I had been thinking about my situation for six hours at this point and saw quite clearly that being contrite, throwing myself on the mercy of the court, and possibly getting disbarred—well, certainly getting disbarred—these were the only things that might keep me out of prison. I knew it was time to change my ways, but I didn't feel it yet. I thought maybe the best thing I could do was not disappoint the client who was coming to see me and be as good a lawyer as I could be. It gave me a terrible, glutinous stomachache to think that this part of my life, practicing law, was drawing to a close and within a year I might instead be locked up in Plainfield or Putnamville like any one of the people I had failed in court. I had been in the corner of so many unlucky men. Surely they would be glad to see me! Or not. There was a good chance that, after failing my clients in court and then charging their families for my services, I might have made some enemies.

It was possible I had only a few weeks of freedom left. The meals I ate in the weeks to come, the women, the love I might or might not find—these were all that I was going to get because the next time I appeared in court, I would be judged.

I went into the tiny bathroom of my office, removed my shirt, and gave myself a good scrubbing with some wet paper towels. I also dropped my pants and washed a bit down there, just on the off chance. It was hard to say, with divorce cases, just what would be on the table and what would be under it. If I was mere weeks away from prison food and joblessness, I would not object if my next client fell in love with me. And I didn't see what harm using my credit card for a steak and martini would do in the meantime. Why deny ourselves the simple joys in life, especially when we see them slipping away forever?

I was not a bad-looking forty years old, after all, and even though I preferred to keep my clothes on a bit longer than I did when I was younger, I still had the luxury of a high metabolism that kept my weight at a tiger-like 210. That was, admittedly, 45 pounds more than I weighed in high school, but I dressed much better now and actually owned my car, though at the moment it was behind a chain-link fence on

Delaware Street. I kept a few spare shirts in my file cabinet and managed to put one on. I was working my chin over with a cordless razor when I heard the electric eye bing in the waiting area, and Tess Parker said my name over the sound of the closing door.

I met her in the hallway outside my office. I had an empty manila folder in my hand. "This way, this way," I said. "I was just finishing something up. I spent most of the day in court." Tess Parker taught junior high English. She had come straight from work and now nodded quietly and stood beside my client chair until I insisted she sit. She was no more than five feet tall but had a nightmarishly statuesque body, one that had caught my attention right away when her friend Judy introduced us. Her looks doubtlessly tormented her students, the females of whom were still budlike and developing and the males not even that. The boys, in the corners of their notebooks, were probably drawing exaggerated caricatures of girls that nevertheless somewhat resembled my client in their sheer excess. Her body was, in short, exactly what lonely fourteen-year-old boys hoped women looked like. I can't remember how I knew her friend Judy, apart from the fact that I had supposedly filed some paperwork on Judy's behalf. I do remember smoking some marijuana with Judy, marijuana she had furnished to pay me for representing her. Apparently she'd told Tess that I was flexible in terms of my billing practices, or maybe I had said something similar.

"Did you say something about dinner?" I said now. "I'm

running on fumes here, to be honest. I've been working all day, no time for a snack even."

"It wasn't too forward of me?" Tess stood again. "I thought it would be a good way to fill you in on why—"

"Of course, of course," I said, "but since I'm hungry for a steak, I insist that you let me take you to Morton's."

"No, I'm inviting you."

I laughed. "Of course not. Anyway, shall we go? Do we have time for a quick drink first? How about Nicky Blaine's?"

"That's fine with me." Tess moved into the hallway. "But didn't you say you were hungry?"

I laughed again and decided to brave it in shirtsleeves since my trial coat was covered with homeless hair and grime from where I'd half-slept against the wall of the county jail. "As your attorney," I said, "I advise you to drink a Cosmopolitan before you say anything else. I'm having a three-olive martini because it's been that kind of day."

She smiled and it was a lovely little smile. I turned out the lights behind us.

Tommy the bartender, when we ordered, confirmed that everyone really did call me Whip. I told Tess that no one called me Karl or Mr. Whipker except my parents or a judge and I had heard quite enough of that for one day, to which she laid an encouraging hand on my arm and asked if I was all right. "Of course I am," I said. "Why wouldn't I be?"

"Because your eyes—you look like you're about to tear up."

I pointed at myself in disbelief and shook my head. "I'm fine," I said. "Tell me about how you know Judy."

"We work together," Tess said. "Did you forget?" And she related a series of school episodes that, quite frankly, I let slip away into the curtained Frank Sinatra ambience. I barely remembered Judy, let alone junior high school, so combining the two into a story made a rather unfair and brutish demand on my concentration and my interest, but at least it was a distraction from thoughts of the Honorable Judge Marsha Wallace.

Tess was wearing a pearl-buttoned blouse tucked into a calico skirt that had deep pockets for red ink pens and attendance slips. When she crossed her legs, I saw her bare shins and cowboy boots, which I found encouraging—as was the immense taper between her chest and waist. Her admittedly distracting proportions were not even three feet away from me atop the leather barstool, and they were certainly not concealed by the way she kept her knees pointed in my direction but swiveled to handle her drink and napkin over the bar. Her story blinked to life when I heard her say something about how she was in even worse financial straits than Judy, though not planning bankruptcy.

"She said you were cool about the billing," Tess ventured. "That you weren't one of those lawyers who was obsessed with money. You did say, on the phone, that if we met you could maybe just give me some advice?"

"Between friends," I said. "Friends help each other out, right?"

"Right." Tess smiled. "And I realize we're more like friends-of-friends, but I'm willing to pay, you know. I just need a little time. Once the divorce goes through, I won't be paying half our mortgage anymore."

"Where will you be living?"

She looked shyly at the floor. "I've got some leads."

"I see." At this point I managed to deliver my usual speech about trust and how quite often in the past I had helped people, which I was glad to do, but always at some time and expense on my part, involving my paralegal and notary as well, only to be treated like an ugly stepbrother once the affair was over. "I remind people of something unpleasant. And no one likes lawyers."

"I would never do that to you," Tess said.

"Tommy," I said to the bartender. "Can you freshen these up? Tess, I believe you. I believe *in* you. But my faith in human nature is a bit tenuous right now. If I were harder on my clients, I could have an office with stained wood and English hunting scenes everywhere—"

"Instead of being next to a tuxedo rental?" Tess finished. "I know. Judy said you were a soft touch."

I smiled and shook my head. I made an effort to appear lost in thought. "Tess, divorces can be ugly, dragged-out things. I understand your husband doesn't know you're talking to me?"

She shook her head.

"I'll need to see some financial statements. For the division of property," I said.

"I don't care about the property," she said. "I just want out."

"Well, not to be crude, but I also need to make sure I am compensated somehow."

She blinked at me.

"We'll work it out," I said, and I raised my glass, which made her raise hers and the glasses touched above our knees. "To freedom," I said.

"Amen," she said. She finished her first Cosmopolitan and moved her new one closer. "God, this is embarrassing, but I don't usually drink much. I've already got to go to the ladies' room."

I pointed her toward the back and she touched my knee when she hopped off her stool. As she crossed the room, Tommy folded his arms on the bar and said, "Good things come in small packages, don't they? She's got a pair of gazon-gas you could build a house on. I'll give you twenty bucks if you can get her to flash her headlights here at the bar."

"Tommy," I said, "my client is a schoolteacher."

"Okay, ten, in that case." Tommy stuffed a towel into a glass and started scrubbing. "I thought she was a college girl."

Two middle-aged tourists came into the bar, one wearing a black baseball cap that said WWJD on the front. "Can you believe that?" I hissed. "Baseball caps in a martini bar."

"Relax," Tommy said.

"What frequency is that, Tommy?" I said, pointing at the hat and my forehead. "WWJD?"

"It's not a radio station," the man in the hat answered. "It stands for What Would Jesus Do? It's something we need to ask ourselves more often. Sir, can I have a Bud Lite?"

Tommy began the beer list with the two strangers, who seemed rather nonplussed because the ten beers available did not include any "LITE" ones, though one of the men seemed to recognize the name "Sam Adams."

I watched the two men talk to each other with their shoulder-to-shoulder familiarity. The one with the ball cap looked about forty. The other man had gray hair on his arms and frowned with a solid, potato-like mustache—so broad, I think, in an attempt to hide his thickening, old man face. I noticed that when Tommy brought them their Sam Adams, the two men closed their eyes for a second before talking again. "Tommy," I whispered, "is it me, or did those two just say grace for two glasses of beer?"

Tommy shrugged. Tess came back and smiled at the two men, which seemed to make them human again. She told me about her soon-to-be ex-husband. I was thinking of my former Bible school teacher. When I'd been the age of Tess's students, this well-intentioned, middle-aged woman had told me Jesus would be the best friend I'd ever have if I'd only let him. Our pastor, a Lutheran with only occasional moments of brilliance, interrupted, "No, He doesn't need anyone's permission. Jesus is there for you. He is your best friend, but it's up to you, whether you recognize him or not. We are always free to be ungrateful." Sitting in Nicky Blaine's was the first time I'd thought about Jesus in years, and all because of that man's baseball cap, which he really shouldn't have been wearing inside anyway.

Tess had made a tiny pile of cherry stems on the bar and was saying that the morning they got married she'd known he wouldn't change, but she had gone along with it, thinking that maybe he would. "But people don't change, do they?" she said. "Not really."

"Sure they do," I said. "Look at you. You're changing your life. This time next year, everything will be completely different."

"I guess you're right."

At that moment, I was horrified by how much my own life might change in the next year. It made me nostalgic. "I was a biology major in college," I said, "and I did a research project on tadpoles. Transformation is really quite commonplace. Look at butterflies."

"You were a biology major?" Tess asked. "That's strange for a lawyer, isn't it?"

"I didn't decide to go to law school until my senior year," I said, though I neglected to mention I had decided against the hard sciences after failing all my classes my freshman year. I had a bachelor's in general studies. I was being half-truthful because I did believe people could change, only I didn't mention that I thought most people changed by getting old and ugly and dead. That didn't seem like a helpful thing to say to a twenty-eight-year-old on the edge of a divorce.

We had three more drinks apiece, or I did; I'm not sure how many she had. We moved to a booth and never got a steak, though Tommy poured a bowl of almonds for us and I was drinking, as I said, martinis large enough to hold three olives and still look silver and pure. The olives were all I needed. Or so I thought, looking at the woman next to me, who was saying something about her husband being in Saint Louis, which I found encouraging, but I also heard the name "Matt," who may or may not have been her husband, I wasn't sure.

I don't remember everything we talked about in that booth, but at one point Tess started crying and I put my arm around her shoulders. And at another point I leaned into her hair and whispered, "Just show them to me. Then I'll know you trust me and I'll be able to trust you."

"I don't think so," she said.

"I'll just have to trust you anyway," I declared. "God, it's the same story every time. But I don't mind. I'll help you."

She nodded.

"I was just kidding," I said. "About, you know, you show-ing me your—"

"I know. I hope so."

I laughed and made a dismissive gesture that really needed a cigarette to be meaningful. She laughed, took a sip of her drink, and then went off to the bathroom again. Tommy gave me a curious look from the bar. We were the only people in the place. "One more apiece," I said, pointing at our glasses, "and then we've got to be going."

Tess was parked outside my office. "You better come up and get some coffee before you drive home," I said. "The police station is right across that parking lot. Come on in. I'm going to make a big pot of joe. I've got some work to do tonight."

She seemed reassured by the idea that I was going to do some more work, as if that made her less drunk herself, though it should have been obvious that I could no more work on a legal brief than I could start to learn cross-stitching at this point in an evening.

We got inside and she sat heavily on the Roman couch in the waiting room. I rummaged for a coffee filter. When I came back into the room, she had capsized, both feet still on the ground, her waist tipped sideways, one elbow over the arm of the couch. I bent above her and lifted her feet onto the couch—with purely gentlemanly intentions because she looked so uncomfortable and drunk. Then, because I didn't want to get dirt on the upholstery, I removed her boots. Her dress had fallen back above her knees, and I might have indulged, just a little, my adolescent curiosity while I had her ankles in my hands. She had much smaller underwear than I ever expected a teacher to wear, but then again she wasn't my teacher. Looking down on her sleeping face, her warm legs in front of me, I was dying of curiosity to see what had been distracting me all evening, what Tommy the bartender called her gazongas, and which, as I said, no doubt tormented the seventh grade boys she worked with. It didn't seem like it would be a complicated operation to have a look, because she had the first two buttons undone, and her shirttail had come out of her skirt at some point in the evening.

I knelt above her, feeling a bit like Dracula, scarcely breathing, her own breath soft against my cheek though with a fragrant candylike smell of Cosmopolitans. My fingers worked thickly, trembling against her rising chest, but then I pulled her unbuttoned shirt open like curtains and was rewarded by just what I expected. It took me a minute to gather my courage and open her bra so that my view of her glories was unobstructed.

I don't feel my conduct with Tess is really something worth discussing in a court of law; we were both consenting adults. I was at least as drunk as she was, although I admit I handled my liquor better. To accuse me of "criminal confinement" or "sexual misconduct" seems unduly harsh. To prove my point, at no time did I ever disrobe myself nor did I physically familiarize myself with the person of Ms. Parker. I only looked! And I saw nothing that would not be common on the beaches of France.

In any case, with her bra down around her stomach, straps tangled in the sleeves of her blouse, and her two breasts unencumbered and free, her face heavy and eyes closed, a moment I'd been waiting for—I was running out of steam. It had been a long, long day and I felt like a broken spring that had been stretched out and refuses to go back to its original shape. I decided maybe I really should ask myself *what would Jesus do?*

The answer I came to was this: if he really was my best friend, he would go out and score me some coke since my car was impounded and I was obviously busy. I had this unhappy, half-naked schoolteacher to think about. I would love to have licked her breasts and then done a line of coke off each one. These were occasions that came all too rarely in life, I knew, and I wasn't sure how to proceed. I wasn't sure I could do anything without a little pick-me-up, and failure was out of the question. One decision I had made early on in the evening was not to disappoint my last remaining client. Unfortunately, thanks to the Honorable Judge Marsha Wallace, my pockets were empty.

I decided that I should take my car and head over to the Red Garter, where the bouncer owed me for defending him on his own possession charges, although the last time I was there, it was true, he had made me pay the cover, but only, I believe, because his boss was watching.

Then I realized, of course, that my car was padlocked behind a thick desk and several meters of concertina wire at 3rd and Delaware. If I hadn't seen Tess Parker's purse on the floor, I don't know what I would have done.

Her softball-sized purse held nothing but her driver's license, some credit cards, Listerine breath strips, and a thick ring of brass and silver keys, one of which was surely for the Nissan Sentra parked out front. As I rattled the keys, I leaned over Tess and asked if I could borrow her car and she quite clearly murmured yes. That she may have called me Matt means nothing because, as I have stated, she had some measure of difficulty accepting the fact that people call me Whip.

And, of course, some would say I should have reassembled her undergarments or her blouse before leaving, but, to be honest, this didn't even cross my mind because I intended to return promptly, for obvious reasons.

I was stopped at the light on Maryland and Meridian when a wine-colored Mercury slid past me, its headlights aglow and the interior a happy aquarium of dashboard light. Of course I recognized the Honorable Judge Marsha Wallace, and though I'd never met him, I supposed the driver to be her husband because he looked roughly her equal in age and stature. I had the windows down on the Sentra and I could hear them singing along to *The Barber of Seville*, of all things. It irritated me to no end that she could be out enjoying herself after being responsible for the longest and worst day of my life even if, it was true, my day was not turning out so badly. I turned left and got behind them, and when we started going east on Washington, out of downtown, I began to flip my brights on and off. Then I cut my lights completely and drove up close behind them and suddenly hit my headlights, laughing maniacally because, understandably, it was a great relief after the day's stress and a lifetime's general frustration with authority. I kept this up for several blocks, but then I was afraid her husband would call the police on his cell phone and anyway I thought it would be more satisfying not just to scare them for a few seconds but to give them something that would be a pain in the ass for days—still not at all a fair trade compared to the aggravation and injury of being charged with felony drug possession when you are in the middle of representing an economically deprived teenager accused of solicitation.

Anyway, I had the brilliant idea of idling on the side of the road, then making a U-turn and hurrying up Washington until I found them again. My plan was to follow them home and maybe drive over their mailbox or through their lawn. My plan wasn't clear at that point. But when I saw them pull into the parking lot of a Village Pantry, I thought it would be delicious to go in after them, let her see me, and then key her car when I left. She'd never be able to prove it was me, of course, but she would know.

And so, at the Village Pantry I parked beside their car and opened the Sentra door a little wide so that it put a matchstick dent in the burgundy-colored Mercury. Then I realized that the husband had gone into the store but the Honorable Judge Marsha Wallace was still sitting in the passenger seat, her aging face a bird's nest of worry. The fluorescent light of a convenience store, even diffused through a window and a windshield, is the most unflattering light of all and can make even the best of us look somehow shriveled or like failures.

In any case, she cocked a finger and her window slid down. "Mr. Whipker," she said. "What on earth do you think you're doing?"

"Why, I'm sorry. Do I know you?" I pressed one hand to my chest and leaned toward her window, which made her slide to the center of the car.

"My husband is inside," she said flatly.

"I don't believe I've had the pleasure," I said.

"Mr. Whipker," she said.

"Yes."

"Why are you here? Why are you following me?"

"I'm here." I waved at the bright window and the rows of overpriced snack foods and toilet paper inside. "To buy something."

"Let me give you some advice," she said, "since we're no longer in a court of law. This is just my opinion, one adult to another, but I think you need to get right with God. You are not making yourself very likable."

And it was at this moment, with her husband coming out the door and the judge looking so much like my mother that it just about broke my heart, that I felt the same disappointment in her eyes, the same tiredness, and I felt, in my own body, a great and sincere desire to change. Because people can change like tadpoles into frogs and maybe even princes. Anything is possible. I saw the truth in all its disarming simplicity there in the bright light of the Village Pantry. Open twenty-four hours with its unflattering, fluorescent clarity, its white glow was like the manger of my own nativity—which is not to say that I was Jesus, but rather that the frowning judge and her husband formed a kind of immaculate Joseph and Mary with their gray-haired couplehood. I was like a shepherd stumbling upon a baby being born. This baby was Jesus, the best friend I had been ignoring, ungrateful as a wretch. And it was at that moment that I decided to stop practicing law and do something useful—to save my own life, with the help of my new and oldest best friend. It was at that moment, standing in front of the Honorable Judge Marsha Wallace—in the pre-midnight parking lot, not the bright light of her courtroom, that I truly felt my life shrink and grow inside me and I had to lean up against my car and try to breathe because I was someone new. I hurried home and went to sleep because I knew the next day would be a big one.

It was at that moment, honestly, and not the next morning when, it turned out, that untrustworthy Tess Parker filed charges on me, charges which really serve no useful purpose because the car is intact and I would be happy to fill it with gas, even. Her husband was out of town so there could have been no real harm done by her waking up in my office. But still, the police came to my door, asking about the Nissan Sentra outside and even though I explained it was all a misunderstanding, there was no reasoning with some people and I can only hope you realize that I mean every word I am saying.

BRANT GILMOUR AND ISA BOONE:
Part 8

Isa and I were at a restaurant called Pizza My Mind when someone said my name. I turned to see K.P., the queen of the YMCA, standing in the doorway. She raised a fist in a salute ("Rock on!" or "Power!" and a half-frightened smile) as she left. Besides yet another pair of sunglasses, she was wearing a winter stocking cap, a bright ski jacket, and tight jeans, and she was elbow to elbow with an equally blond, equally bright-smiling friend. Even with stocking caps on, they looked like their lives might be a giant shampoo commercial. I knew Isa would hate them, but I was unprepared for the silence that greeted me after the door shut and K.P. and her friend were gone. "What?" I said.

"Oh, forget it," Isa said. "You want me to leave so you can chase down the mouseketeer?"

There was something about the way she said it, something gratuitously vicious, that made me want to stick up for K.P., who had done nothing wrong but be nice to me and be pretty. And maybe a part of me did want to join K.P. and her friend in a crowded booth and share a pizza with someone who ate from hunger and not boredom.

"What's a mouseketeer?" I said. "Jesus, how old are you, Isa?"

Isa turned and was gone before I could pull my hands out of my pockets to catch the shutting door. I hesitated before chasing her, which was when I think I knew that things were beginning to end.

I got to thinking about Isa, and, to be honest, about K.P., and I was bitter about a lot of things. Because I was happy with Isa, but it didn't seem like she was always happy with me, and it seemed there were more and more things I wanted to do that Isa was completely disinterested in, not just like mountain biking or anything, but like traveling in Spain. ("Do they have good burritos there?" she'd asked.) Whenever I asked her to do something outside her comfort zone, she would say, "Why don't you ask one of your other friends? That kind of shit just doesn't interest me."

And I would say something like, "I don't have any other friends since we started dating."

"And that's my fault?" she'd say. And I had to admit it wasn't. I hadn't left college with dozens of friends. I'd never had a lot of friends. My best friend was in the Peace Corps and sent back occasional letters full of weird stains on paper that was this odd European size. He was in the Philippines and when I ran into his mother at the Keystone Mall, she showed me a picture of him standing beside a split and burning pesticide barrel with gray fish roasting on a grill. He was so tan and unshaven I almost didn't recognize him.

In college he had written a paper about Matthew Arnold that I used to tease him about.

"How is that going to change the world?" I'd say, and he'd laugh.

"Poetry," he said, "is the world to me."

But there he was, living on the other side of the earth. There were three or four Filipinas in the picture, any one of whom might have been in love with him from the way they were smiling. A short, thick-legged Filipino man with scarred shins was standing nearby, his shirt open and a sharp stick in hand. I guessed this was Eduardo, whom my friend described in his letters as his new blood brother, a man with a passion for tequila and surfing films. I mentioned my friend and the Philipines to Isa and she reacted like I'd mentioned wanting to go to veterinary school.

"What is it?" I said.

"Nothing," she said. But later she added, "How are you going to get your ten years in with the state if you quit to go surfing with your friends in Singapore or wherever?"

Ten years was the magical number, after which an institutional teacher was vested in the state retirement system and could eventually draw a pension. Every year after that increased the amount you could draw and brought the year you could draw it that much closer, so it was a kind of career black hole no one escaped from. But I'd often said, "Oh, fuck that," which made Isa both beam with pride for me and shake her head.

She was ten years older than me, but Plainfield was not

her first job, so Isa was still three years away from being vested herself. She didn't consider losing her retirement to go surfing in the Philippines a good idea. "My dad didn't have a car lot," she said. "He was in the Army. He retired at fifty-five and then was a worthless pain in the ass the rest of his short drunk life. I've got to work for a living."

I wasn't sure why she was so angry, but then she shrugged and said, "You're breaking up with me, aren't you? I can tell."

I said no, no way. And she sighed and said she was tired. Maybe we could meet up the next day? But the next day, she didn't come to work and when I went by her apartment, she wouldn't come to the door.

The following day she was at work, but we didn't see each other much. "Isa," I said, "we've got to talk. Why are you acting like this?"

"You tell me, Brant," she said, "or do you want to ask Barbie at the gym why a woman might act this way? She's probably got lots of good ideas she'd like to share with you."

"Isa," I said. "I don't even know you when you act like this."

"Then you don't know me," she said, "because I always act like this."

I stayed away from Isa for a few days. Saturday morning, I worked out in the empty weight room of the Y and drove to Plainfield and parked outside Isa's Pepperidge Farm apartment. I went up to her door and no one answered, but

I heard her inside. "I'm not going anywhere," I said. "I'm going to climb up the balcony if you don't open up."

"Don't even think about it, you dumb ass," I heard her say. Then it occurred to me, from the tone of her voice, that I had once seen a gun in her apartment. I realized Isa wasn't some girl I knew from college. And I wasn't going to climb up the balcony. She finally came to the door. She looked terrible. "What?" she said.

"We've got to talk," I said.

"Is it him?" a voice said. I looked over her shoulder, past her tangled hair, and I saw Englehart in her kitchen holding a box of Captain Crunch. He wasn't wearing a uniform like I'd always seen him in. He was wearing blue jeans and a Toby Keith T-shirt. He looked fat.

"You're kidding me," I said.

"Brant," Isa said. "I'm sorry."

"Don't be," I said. "I guess we don't need to talk."

I was suddenly on the sidewalk in front of the building. The tangled shrubs looked as familiar as old pets. It made me sad to think I wouldn't be walking up that grainy sidewalk again.

"Oh, who are you kidding? Brant, you so-holy, so-full-of-yourself asshole!" Isa shouted from her balcony. "You were going to break up with me and you know it!"

"What?" I said suddenly, turning to her. "How do you know that? Why him?"

"Why him? Why not?" Isa said. She had her arms crossed. The patio door was shut behind her. Englehart was nowhere in sight. I was alone on the sidewalk. I started to move beneath her, like a goofy Hoosier Romeo, until she covered her face. "He disgusts me. You disgust me. Brant! How did I know? Because I know, Brant. One thing I know about people. They will always fuck up a good thing."

BRANT GILMOUR:
Mike Tyson Slept Here

Johnny Winston had been an officer at Plainfield during the Mike Tyson era. He told three stories to newcomers like Englehart, and Englehart told them to me before we stopped being friends.

"Here are my three Mike Tyson stories," Winston had said. "One time he came in the chow hall when I was working. This little black guy I had ladling soup didn't say a word until Tyson was gone, then he came over to me and whispered, 'I used to whip him on Nintendo Punch-Out.' And one time someone did try to fight him, I guess, over in the dorm. I had an offender tell me about it. I asked what happened and my guy said, 'Tyson hit him.' I guess he threw one punch and the guy was out. His friends carried the guy to his bunk and the guy woke up in the middle of the night and thought he was dead. But I also know that Worstell, who used to teach science in the school here, once told me Tyson had asked him 'If we shot a rocket at the sun at night, would it burn up?' And I asked Worstell about this and he swore three times it happened."

When Winston told this to Englehart, they were standing in the foyer of the school. Herbert was there, cleaning the heat register with a gray rag. During his first week of OJT, Englehart had been told to find the school maintenance worker and get the school looking good because the commissioner was coming to visit. Englehart was told specifically to make sure the heat registers were clean because the superintendent himself had noticed how filthy the vents were. Herbert, the inmate worker, had shaken his head, saying he'd be glad to do it, no problem, but there was little chance he'd get them all done himself in one afternoon. "You give me a hand, we could maybe do it. What if you did the right side of the hallway and I do the left?"

Englehart, his first month on the job, had agreed, and it was only three hours later when he realized that Herbert's side of the hallway had only three registers but his own had fourteen because that was the side of the building the furnace was on. He had never forgotten this, so whenever he saw Herbert standing idle, Englehart made the inmate grab a rag and clean.

One afternoon a few months after Englehart's conversation with Johnny Winston, Herbert shuffled up to the officer's booth and said, "You know, I was here the first time back in '93, when Tyson was here, and we were in GED class together a few weeks until he quit. I got mine."

"That right?" Englehart said. "You're bullshitting me, ain't you?"

"No," Herbert said. "I got me a GED."

"No, about Tyson."

"We had ourselves a real good teacher, man named Herbert. No relation of mine."

"He white?"

"He staff. What you think?"

"So you guys pass notes in class? You and Tyson best buds?"

"No, I never spoke to the man. But we read some fine books I'll never forget. We read *How to Kill a Mockingbird* by Miss Harvard Lee. Yes. And I remember one conversation we had in class. Our teacher asked if we liked the book and Mike, he didn't say nothing—oh, he never said nothing in class—and the teacher, he called on him, and said, 'Mike, you like it?' and Tyson said he sure did. 'Why?' the teacher asked him. And Tyson said, 'Because I'm Tom Robinson.'"

Englehart listened, then nodded. "Heh, I think we read that in high school. You got to go tell Gilmour. He's all up into books and shit." Englehart reached over and hit the intercom to my room. "Brant, come up here a minute. You got to hear this."

I came to the front and Herbert told me the story. I looked at them both and said, "That's got to be the most disturbing thing I've ever heard."

"You young," Herbert said.

Englehart asked loudly: "Who was Tom Robinson again?"

"Tom Robinson was completely innocent," I said. "Of rape. And everything else. Of everything."

"Let's fire his ass," Englehart said, pointing at Herbert eagerly.

I hadn't let him at the time. Herbert and I shared a look of disbelief at Englehart's expense. Then one day half a year later, I was thinking about that conversation and called Herbert up to my desk. I knew he was no professional predator like Mike Tyson, but he was no Tom Robinson either. "I don't think I need you up here anymore," I said, and I cut him from my work line. He gathered up his things and left without a sound. The truth was I'd gotten tired of Herbert. I didn't like the way he spoke to me as if I were dumber than him. Or maybe it was this more than anything else: he talked to me as if we were friends. I watched his plastic bag full of papers leave the room. He didn't stop in the doorway, didn't look back. Afterward, I felt a certain amount of shame.

BRANT GILMOUR AND K.P.

We decided to meet at the Old Point Tavern, where I had gone with Pearl that time or two and which I was surprised to find out K.P. knew quite well. "I know the bartender," she said. "He's gay, but he says he won't work another queer bar on account of there's too much whining."

"That sounds like self-hatred to me."

"Oh, Billy hates everyone except himself. So I don't know about that."

I got there first and sat at the bar, which was dim and wood, beneath a stamped linoleum ceiling and with a tangle of white Christmas lights strung among dusty bottles above a long mirror. The bartender had a lean, harsh face and an entire newspaper of tattoos up his two arms, intricate ribbons of words and smoky shapes. He looked like some kind of Celtic killer, but when I said I was meeting K.P. he smiled at me for half a second, and then he wanted to shake my hand. "Are you really?" he said. When K.P. came in the door, I reached for my wallet, but he waved it away. "First one's on me," he said.

"Two of my favorite men in the world," K.P. said. "You met?"

"I've seen him in here before," Billy said, turning to me. "You probably don't remember. Look—if this one isn't smiling the next time she comes in, you ain't ever drinking here again. You understand?"

"Your mission. If you choose to accept it," K.P. said, and she smiled wide, in such a way that it seemed like a landscape picture, not a portrait. It seemed completely effortless and genuine, but then it lasted long enough for me to know she was nervous too. I wanted to smile magically like she did. I wasn't sure if she was smiling at me or at Billy, but that didn't seem to matter so much, in that I felt like I'd spent months snickering or chuckling but had not smiled with my entire face since I'd started in the prison.

"I accept," I said.

It was nine at night. There was no reason for her to wear sunglasses, so K.P. sat at the bar with her dim side far from me. "So how often do you work out?" she asked, and we talked about nothing important for half an hour.

K.P. put one elbow on the bar and leaned forward. It was early enough in the evening that the wooden bar was still glossy, and for a second she was reflected beneath herself, like a Hoosier queen of hearts with a bottle of Amstel Light. She took a drink and seemed to weigh things. Her unmoving eye reserved judgment, but when she said, "So you work at the prison that used to hold Mike Tyson?" her voice seemed artificially happy, as if she were vigorously shaking hands on an uncertain bet. "What's that like?"

"Oh, it's a job," I said.

"You ever meet him?"

"You know? He left, and now he never writes, never calls . . ."

Like I said, I had collected the Plainfield Mike Tyson stories, but I didn't know what I could tell this woman with her long legs twined into the barstool beside mine. I had a theory I'd shared with Isa once, that we were all Mike Tyson: gruesome inside but with voices like little birds, and we hurt people for no good reason except that it was a living, and it seemed some of us, like Tyson, were powerful and lucky and invincible until suddenly we weren't.

Isa had laughed at me. "Grow up," she said. "News flash: Life's not fair."

So when someone pretty and bright-haired, like K.P., asked me about the prison or about Mike Tyson, it was mildly embarrassing. I had a million things I could say, but they were all dead rabbits I'd be cleaning at the table. They were conversation killers. K.P. leaned on one elbow and smiled like we were back in the gym. I suddenly pictured her with fewer, tighter clothes on. I wanted to know her, but it seemed impossible. She was on the next stool, a million miles away. She didn't seem like she could possibly know what failure or sadness was. She didn't work in a prison.

It made me think of Pearl, which made me sad, and I looked at K.P.—this tall blonde girl who worked out five times a week—and I wondered what kinds of things ever made her sad. "K.P.," I said, "tell me the most embarrassing thing that's ever happened to you."

She smiled. "Not after one drink. How about you?"

I thought about telling K.P. about my sister, or about Pearl, or about any one of a number of things, but then I felt like I'd told all those stories before. I could have told her about Dennis Herbert or about the khaki-suited students that made up my classes, but I wanted to step outside the prison and talk about the other flickering moments that made up my life, if I still had one.

"My last girlfriend is with my former best friend now. I ran into them at Wal-Mart a week ago. I still work with her. He doesn't work there anymore. They were buying some groceries and when they saw me, I could tell they both hated me."

"I'd think they'd be embarrassed, not you." K.P. squinted at my face. "Or—why? Did you hurt them? Both?"

"Maybe so."

"That's not embarrassment," K.P. declared. "You felt embarrassed? I'd think you'd feel like an asshole."

"Well, I did. I did. I guess I'm mixing up ashamed and embarrassed."

"Yeah, that was ashamed. Embarrassed is when—I'll tell you the difference." K.P. cleared her throat. "My most embarrassing moment? When I was fifteen I had a mad crush on my English teacher. I thought about him all the time. He wore corduroy blazers, which I though was sophisticated. And he kept this tree branch, this bare wooden stick on his desk because he thought it was beautiful. This teacher always made a big fuss if we came to class unprepared and he had to loan us a pencil or paper or anything. One day I finally got so desperate, I pretended to lose the pencil he gave me because I wanted to keep it. He kept me after class, which I loved, of course. Me and my best friend, who hadn't done her homework, and he told her to write 'I will bring my homework on time' a hundred times, and he told me he wanted me to write 'I will take care of Mr. Michaelson's pencils as if they were my children' fifty times. I didn't care. I would have written it five hundred times if I could have just sat there and watched him erase the chalkboard. He was only like twenty-two and this was his first year teaching."

"That was your most embarrassing moment?" I asked.

"No. As soon as he told me to write, I raised my hand. 'I don't have a pencil,' I said, 'so how can I write?'"

"'Here,' he said, and he—all dramatic—slams this brand-new pencil down in front of me. But then he says, 'Now keep your eye on this one—' and he stops talking and I realize he's staring at me, at my—" K.P. pointed at her glass eye. "And he can't recover. He just mouths the air and then says, 'Don't lose it,' and he turns away and I burst out crying and he apologizes. My best friend was watching the whole thing and I never got over it, really. I didn't do any more English homework the rest of the time I was in high school. I'm lucky I can read a newspaper."

"I'm an English teacher," I said. "I hope you won't hold it against me."

"English teachers are my kryptonite," K.P. said. Her lips formed a smile, and she raised her beer bottle to hide it.

"What about a shameful moment?"

"I don't know if I want to tell you that just now," she said. She looked wistfully at the dim shadow of herself in the bar mirror. The tattooed bartender floated past our images like some kind of demon. The Christmas lights made the bar resemble a kind of faerieland, and K.P. was almost talking to herself or to the image in the mirror when she said, "But I've done things I'm ashamed of. We move on, right?"

"That's not what prison's about," I said. "We don't always get to move on."

"What's the prison way?" she asked. "Tell me."

"Maybe I will," I said, "but it will take a while."

"Well, second round's on me." K.P. caught the bartender's eye. "Billy, come here a minute. You might want to hear this."

K.P. put her hand on my forearm. Her fingers were warm. When she leaned forward I could feel the warmth of her face. Her hair was glimmering with an invisible crown made by the Christmas tree lights.

"I like the way you look at me," K.P. said. She smiled again. Billy leaned one hip against the bar and stared at me patiently. His green and blue arms looked snakelike and dangerous. "Billy," K.P. said, "Brant works out at Plainfield. At the prison. He's going to tell us what he's learned in prison."

I took a breath. And then I started talking.

ABOUT THE AUTHOR

Chris Huntington holds an MFA from Bennington College. He spent almost ten years working for the Indiana Department of Correction. His writing has been has been anthologized in *This I Believe II: More Personal Philosophies of Remarkable Men and Women* and *Mamas and Papas: On the Sublime and Heartbreaking Art of Parenting.* He currently lives in China with his wife and son.